Also by Shontaiye
All 4 Da Doe
All 4 Da Doe 2
Deceit, Lies, & Alibi's
Through The Eyes of a Hoodrat

Coming Soon by Shontaiye
Through The Eyes of a Hoodrat 2
Thru the Eyes of a Jackboy
Blood 4 My Brother
Wrong Turn

Contact us:
Uptown Books @ uptownbookspublications.com
uptownbookspublication@yahoo.com
uptownshontaiye@yahoo.com
twitter.com/LaRekaShontaiye

Deceit, Lies, & Alibis 2

SHONTAIYE

Uptown Books
1147 S. Salisbury Boulevard
Suite 8-191
Salisbury, MD, 21801

This is a work of fiction. All of the characters, organizations, and events portrayed in this novel are either products of the author's imagination or are used fictitiously.

Deceit, Lies, & Alibi's 2. Copyright © 2015 Uptown Books. All rights reserved. No part of this book may be used or reproduced in any manner whatsoever without written permission except in the case of brief quotations embodied in critical articles or reviews.

ISBN-13: 978-0-9863212-4-5
ISBN-10: 0-9863212-4-9

ACKNOWLEDGMENTS

I just want to express appreciation to the people that have actually read my book. I appreciate that you took the time to read a novel by an unknown author. Thank you to my mama who gives me honest feedback, my daughter Tatyana for listening to my ideas, and last but not least my family for being supportive.

DECEIT, LIES, AND ALIBIS 2

ONE

Shaleea

"I'M NOT TRYING to do anything. And as you can see, I'm a big girl, and I can handle whatever consequence come with what I do."

Shaleea remembered saying those words but wished she could now take them back. She had fucked up big time. She didn't look back but felt Mann's naked muscular body pressed against hers. She too was naked. Her head throbbed and her weave lay wild and untamed against the white hotel pillow case. Somehow they had ended up in the bed.

She didn't remember the whole night, only vague parts. She remembered feeling really good.

She wasn't sure if it was because she felt wanted or if it was because she was engaging in something forbidden; her fiancée's best friend. Shaleea slowly and quietly crawled out of the bed so she wouldn't wake Mann.

"Hey, where you going?" he asked. She froze. She had hoped he stayed sleep. The situation was so awkward.

"Hey. I'm just going to get myself together," she replied quietly. She didn't turn around to face him.

He reached and gently grabbed her arm, stopping her from getting up. "How you feeling?" he asked with genuine concern. He hoped she felt how he felt.

"I'm okay," she replied. She already knew what he was asking. He wanted to know how she was feeling about the two of them; what had just happened.

"We need to talk…I was thinking we could go to breakfast," he suggested.

"I don't know about that—" she started, but Mann quickly cut her off.

"I mean, I know we can't go anywhere around here, but we can drive out somewhere and talk there. Listen, I don't want you to worry about anything ok," he stated. "I know this situation is kind of fucked up but at the same time it was beautiful," he said, trying to persuade her to view things how he did.

"Yeah but Noah is going to fucking go ballistic if he—"

"Man fuck—"He paused abruptly and took a deep breath. "Listen, I'm a man first. I can hold my own. And you don't have to worry about shit either." He was about to say fuck Noah but that wouldn't have been a good look. She did love Noah after all. Her brain was probably already doing somersaults and he didn't want her to get defensive. Shaleea was vulnerable and he would play on that until he got her where he wanted her; with him.

Noah

Noah climbed out of the bed feeling slightly disoriented. He figured he probably had too much to drink the night before. He had been drinking a lot more lately since Shaleea was still giving him grief. He looked to his side and saw Eve sleeping peacefully. He rolled his eyes at her and foolishly thought about suffocating her while she slept. However, he wasn't trying to go to jail. He pulled himself out of the bed and prepared to leave. He would shower when he was home.

He didn't bother to wake Eve up. He threw on his clothes and boots and took the back way out of the cheap motel. As he walked to his truck he reached into his pocket and pulled out his phone to call Shaleea. Of course she didn't answer but he didn't care. He was about to end the games very soon. He planned to go to her mother Gina's house and see if she was there. He would make his rounds one by one until he found her. He knew a lot of what he did wasn't right but he loved Shaleea and wasn't going to continue sitting around like a sad dog. He had to do something.

Mann

Mann already knew Noah was soon going to be a major issue in his life. He knew that he had crossed the line by sleeping with Shaleea, let alone contemplating pursuing her for himself. He knew that eventually the truth would surface and Noah would want to war with him. *So be it*, he thought, before looking up at Shaleea. He was far from pussy and would wreck whoever if necessary.

"What you thinking about over there," he asked Shaleea. She was being extremely quiet and it was making him nervous. They had been at the quaint diner for quite some time and she had barely said a word.

"What we did was fucked up Mann," she blurted out. "I was drinking and I let my emotions cloud my judgement. What I did was out of spite and I don't want to come between you and Noah. Yall been friends for a long time." Tears welled up in her dark eyes as she sat and analyzed the damage that she had done. She used her fork to continue to pick at her uneaten breakfast.

"I know it's a lot to absorb but everything does happen for a reason. I mean you two are separated, and you have been living apart in a hotel for several months."

"True," she said, lowering her eyes back down to her plate.

"I'm not trying to step on Noah's toes, cuz he

is my nigga, but I think this could be something bigger. Now I know you used to Noah taking care of you and having money at your disposal but I could do that too," he exaggerated. He had money but not the kind of money Noah did. He would real soon though after putting in a little work.

She looked up at Mann and gave a half-smile. It wasn't about the money with her. The two of them just couldn't be. Noah would go insane and probably try to kill them both. In another life, Mann would be an ideal mate; but this wasn't that life, and if they wanted to continue living in it, they would have to put an end to what they had begun.

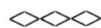

Mann pulled up to his new home and turned off his Charger. He looked over at Shaleea and smiled. He hoped she liked it.

"This the new house ya real estate friend hooked me up with. I've been in it for a few weeks now," he smiled.

When he took her to breakfast he purposely drove thirty minutes outside the city to the small town of Blue Bell, Pennsylvania where he had just purchased a house for him and his grandmother. He wanted her to see it so she could get an idea of what he could give her.

Shaleea looked at the house and was impressed. It was beautiful. It was a single story home but it had a beautiful wrap around porch and gorgeous, colorful landscaping.

"This is beautiful Mann. Steve really hooked you up," she gushed, while continuing to marvel at the home and neighborhood. It actually made her miss her own home more.

"You wanna see inside," he asked. He didn't wait for an answer before opening up the door and hopping out.

"Yeah sure," she mumbled, and exited out of the car.

They walked into the home and Shaleea found it was just as lovely inside as it was out, with up-to-date fixtures throughout.

"I wanted a two story but my grandmother can't walk up the steps too well. I want her to be comfortable and able to enjoy it all without getting too tired," he explained.

"Well that was thoughtful of you," she said,

still admiring the home.

After looking around the house Shaleea asked Mann to take her to pick up her car. She had to pick up Heaven and check on the laundromats to ensure everything was running smoothly. Mann agreed since he too had some business to handle. He enjoyed the short time he spent with Shaleea but had to go since Noah had been calling and texting him non-stop most of the morning. Lately they had been in talks about buying more product and Noah wanted to go over the financial aspects of everything.

Mann pulled up to the parking lot where they left Shaleea's car the previous night near the club. Without thinking Mann jumped out with Shaleea and walked her the short distance to where her gray Camaro was parked.

"So am I gon see you again?" Mann asked, getting straight to the point.

"I don't know if that's a good idea Mann. I want things to go back to normal and for us to remain friends," she said as sweetly as possible.

"Why I get the feeling you going back to Noah," he asked, seemingly jealous.

Shaleea grew quickly irritated since she had

already told him she didn't know what she was going to do. He basically wanted her to choose between the two of them, which to her was a bit absurd.

"Mann, look. You a cool ass dude. You are, but me and you can't be. It would be bad. You know that. Our circumstances won't allow us to be. I mean—I love Noah..." she said sincerely, while making eye contact with Mann so he wouldn't misunderstand what she was saying.

"I don't know what I'm going to do honestly. I may go back eventually...I may not. I don't know. But whatever choice I make, I can't be with you. It's just something that I can't do."

"I can dig it," Mann said. He wasn't trying to here any of what she just said. He would get what he wanted.

TWO

Noah

"What's up bull? Where you been, I been calling you all morning nigga?" Noah asked through the receiver of his iPhone. He was a little irritated that he had to call and text Mann several times before he finally called back. He wasn't used to being on hold for anyone. Noah had been mainly business lately and when he was ready to discuss it, he didn't like getting the run around from anyone, Mann included.

Fucking ya wifey, Mann wanted to say in response to Noah's question. After sleeping with Shaleea Mann's already mediocre feelings for Noah changed instantly. He really dug Shaleea and he felt like she deserved better. Most of all, he wanted her for himself. Some nigga's had it all and didn't deserve it; Noah was one of them. Mann was grimey at its best and he had every intention of rocking Noah to sleep if he became any sort of problem in his life. He didn't give a fuck. He would get whatever he wanted no matter who had to pay the price. He was just that type of boy. Of course he wouldn't be stupid and immediately say "fuck Noah." He would wait until he no longer needed him.

"My damn phone had died. I hit you back as soon as I got home and put it on the charger," he answered.

"Oh. You musta been creeping last night. Let me find out you was laid up all night wit a hoe." Noah laughed jokingly.

"Naa my nigga. I don't do hoes. This jawn was right. Shawty was bad. Thick as fuck with good pussy... Had a nigga wanting to move her in and put some babies up in her," he said, disrespecting Noah intentionally without him knowing.

"Oh yeah," Noah responded. "Well they don't come often, so you better cuff her," he said with a laugh.

"I intend to," Mann stated casually.

The two men made plans to meet later, but first Noah had to handle a few important things.

Noah bobbed his head to Kevin Gates latest song and waited for Shaleea to pull up to her mother's house. It was Soul Food Sunday and he knew she would be showing up to eat with her family. After about another thirty minutes of waiting, she finally pulled up. He mashed his blunt out into the ash tray and looked at her as she walked up. She had on a pink Victoria's Secret sweat suit, and wore her hair up in a messy bun. Before she could walk up the steps to Gina's home he started up the car and drove up closer to the house, honking twice so she would notice it was him.

Shaleea stopped to look and quickly recognized Noah, however, she didn't recognize the car. Instantly she knew what he was up to. She rolled her eyes.

"Hey bae," he said with a smile, before stepping out of the car and quickly approaching her. He looked at her and then pointed to the brand new 2015, all white Audi Q56. "That's yours. An early Christmas gift," he said, hoping she liked it. He wanted to make the conversation quick since it was cold out.

"Thanks but no thanks," she replied smugly, before continuing to walk up the steps. She wasn't impressed. Before she could make it to the top Noah gently grabbed her arm.

"Yo come here, come here," he said, turning her to face him. She huffed and waited for him to talk. "Look, I know that I haven't been the best, but I promise to change. I want you to take the truck and I want you to come home," he said with sincerity.

Shaleea let out another huff and turned around to face him. *Damn I love him*, she thought, as she looked into his eyes for some sign of sincerity. She saw a glimmer of hope.

"I don't know Noah. You always say you gon change but I don't see you doing anything but making me look like a fool. You think I care about a car?" she asked him. "I don't care about that. I have a car and besides my future is very promising and I will eventually be able to buy whatever the fuck I want my damn self. So don't come over here thinking you can buy your way back into my life. I want a man, not gifts!" she said sternly, before walking off up the steps and into the house.

Noah felt defeated. He wanted to grab her by that bun and throw her ass in the truck. However, he didn't want to cause a scene in front of Gina's house. He wasn't sure what else to do. Shaleea was being very stubborn and truthfully she had every right to be. He knew there was no sense in buying anything else and he was contemplating taking back the expensive $50,000 truck. He wasn't into spending frivolously and the purchase was extremely extravagant for Noah who was still quite frugal. He would wait though, he had another idea.

Later that day Noah pulled up to the very nice, two story colonial stone home of his former friend Hakim. He had stopped by to check on Nikka and the kids to make sure they were doing okay and to ensure that they wanted for nothing.

"Uncle Noahhhh," Hakim's youngest child

Xavier called to him in a songlike manner. Xavier was five years old and was cute with a chocolatey complexion like his dad. He had on an Iron Man shirt and his black Jordan's were on the wrong feet. Noah laughed and quickly got out of the car. He scooped Xavier up and hugged his nephew. When Hakim passed, he vowed to remain a permanent fixture and positive male figure in the boy's lives.

"Hey little man! How you been?" Noah asked, swinging him around before putting him down.

"I'm good Uncle Noah, where've you been, and I thought you said you were going to take me to see the "mouse man." Noah had told the boys he was going to take them to Chuckie Cheese but it had innocently slipped his mind.

"Awww, my fault buddy, I forgot. How about you get your brother and if it's okay with your mom, I'll take you both now." Noah didn't mind. It was Sunday and it wasn't like he had anything to do.

"But Xavier, you gotta do one thing for me before we leave," Noah said with a serious face, while leaning down to lower himself to the child's level.

DECEIT, LIES, AND ALIBIS 2

"What?" he asked with his eyes wide, excited that he was about to go to the kiddie arcade with his favorite uncle.

"You gotta put them shoes on the right feet! Swag 101, girls don't like boys with mismatch clumsy feet," he whispered before laughing. Xavier giggled and ran back into the house to get his older brother Hakim Jr. who was busy playing on his Xbox.

"Nikka!" Noah yelled, while walking into the house. As usual the place was impeccably clean and warm, while pleasant smells emanated from the kitchen.

"Hey Noah," Nikka smiled, wiping her wet hands on a towel to dry them. She looked very pretty with her hair up in a knotted bun and a Chinese bang covering her eyes. "I just finished making the boys some lasagna. You want some?"

"Hell yeah. I ain't had a home-cooked meal since—" He stopped himself.

Nikka looked at him and felt a bit sorry for him. She knew he loved Shaleea and she knew that she still hadn't come back. She and Shaleea had become a bit closer after Hakim passed since Shaleea consistently reached out to check on her and the kids.

"How are you?" she asked, seriously. "I know you come by here to check and make sure I'm good but how are you holding up?" she asked. He knew what she was asking, and it wasn't in regards to Hakim.

"I've been better," he admitted. "I'm just empty you know," he said before taking a seat at the built in kitchen bar. "From everything. Losing Hakim. Losing Shaleea…I try to fill my life with people I love. You, the kids, but I'm missing her and Heaven. She don't see it but I love her a lot. She's my world. I don't want to lose her. I don't want to lose anyone else," he said with sincerity. If he was a bitch nigga he would cry, he thought. But he was a G and he refused to let tears escape his eyes.

"I'll talk to her," Nikka said. "I know we aren't the closest but she'll value a female opinion. You just gotta wake up. Look what Hakim lost. You may not lose in the same way, but ultimately you will still lose. Is she worth losing?" she questioned.

"Not at all," he answered.

"Well show her," Nikka said, ending the

conversation by sliding Noah a plate of lasagna with some garlic bread and a glass of tea. "Eat up you gon need your energy to keep up with them bad ass boys. They told me you taking them to Chuckie Cheese."

"Yeah soon as I finish eating and Xavier figure out which shoe go on which foot," he laughed.

Shaleea

Although she had her knee length pea coat wrapped around her body tightly for added warmth, the crisp air felt refreshing against Shaleea's face as she made her way up the manicured walkway of her home.

It had been several months since Shaleea had been to the home her and Noah shared, and the warm feeling it brought to her confirmed that she truly missed being there. After speaking with Nikka the night before, she decided to go and talk with Noah. Nikka had reached out to Shaleea after Noah had taken the boys to Chuckie Cheese. Although she knew Nikka's opinion about cheating would be biased because Nikka had willingly endured it so long, she decided to listen to someone who knew and loved Noah like she did.

She didn't know how the conversation with Noah would go, but she did know that eventually a decision would need to be made; she had been gone for several months. She reasoned with herself that she would either work on reparation with Noah, or make peace with the life they had and move on. She did know that no one was perfect and she was all too familiar with how it felt to have to live with a mistake. To her however, sleeping with Mann was a mistake, but Noah's constant cheating was a choice. Because of Noah's past actions she didn't feel bad about what she had done, since she had only done what she'd done because of his actions. What worried her most was that while she could control what she did, she couldn't control Mann.

Shaleea used her key to let herself in and was shocked at what she saw. Empty bottles of Hennessey were scattered throughout the living room floor, while several empty pizza boxes accompanied them. The house was downright filthy. She walked into the kitchen and saw dishes filling the sink and nets quietly buzzing around them. Shaleea made her way to the bedroom and prayed Noah was alone. She hoped he hadn't stooped to the ultimate level of disrespect by bringing another bitch into the home that carried both their names on the deed.

"Noah," she called after pushing the door open. She breathed a sigh of relief once she saw he was alone. However her heart instantly ached when she saw him passed out sleep on the floor. He hadn't even made it to the bed. A small trashcan that contained vomit stood beside him. She knew he had at some point been in a drunken stupor.

Shaleea got out her phone and called Merry Maids, a cleaning franchise that she used several times a year for her heavy duty cleaning. She had quickly decided that several months of filth was not going to be cleaned up by her. After arranging for them to come out in the morning, Shaleea once again tried to wake up Noah.

"Noah," she quietly called again. This time he opened his eyes and abruptly turned over. He was happy to see her but knew he looked like shit. He definitely felt like it.

"Hey bae," he looked up and whispered

hoarsely, before gently lying his head back down on the floor.

"Noah, you gotta get up and get yourself together. I have the cleaning company on the way… and we need to talk."

Noah slowly pushed himself up to his feet. He had been waiting months to sit down with her and he felt a glimmer of hope fill his chest. He was ready to put all the bullshit behind him and change. Even though he had been with Eve several nights before, he was ready to put a stop to everything if she came home. If he could get her back he wouldn't lose her again. He would make her happy.

THREE

Eve

Eve dialed Noah's number again and listened to the message that was playing to make sure she heard it correctly. *"The number you have called is not in service. Please check the number and try your call again."*

She slammed her phone down in anger before lying back on the faded hotel comforter. It had been over a month since she saw Noah and now his phone was disconnected. She was livid. She wasn't too worried though. His laundromat locations were public and she would eventually run into him sooner or later. Truthfully she didn't have the energy to chase Noah down; figuratively speaking and literally. She had been throwing up all morning and hadn't been able to keep much down except some ginger ale and crackers. She knew her pregnancy wasn't going to be in easy one. She couldn't wait to share the news with Noah. She already knew how he was going to take it.

He'll hate me for a while, but eventually he'll learn to love me, she thought. The baby would eventually bring them together; just like she had planned.

Shaleea

Shaleea walked into the small soul food café on Cheltenham Avenue and quickly looked around. She smiled when she saw her sister Shameka sitting at a small table in a corner by the window.

"Hey Meek," she said, as she approached the table and sat down.

"Hey girl. Bout time you got here, I'm hungry as shit and you was taking forever," she complained.

"Whatever. Ain't nobody tell you to bring ya ass early," Shaleea responded. "I told you 12 o clock, and it's 12:05," she stated, placing emphasis on the times.

"We waiting on Naomi anyway. She'll be here shortly."

"I'm not waiting on her ass. You are. I'm bout to order something to eat," Shameka responded bluntly before picking her menu back up off the table.

Shaleea laughed in amusement at her sister. Shameka was very forward and outspoken just like her other sister Shanita. The only thing was Shameka had even less patience and was quick to—as she put it, put her paws on a bitch.

Shameka was a cute, plump, but very curvy chick. She always had a head full of wavy curls and kept a pair of four inch heels on. However, she was quick to kick them off and go in the trunk of her Dodge Durango and pull out her Air Force One's if she had to check a bitch.

"There Naomi go now," Shaleea stated, looking over to the door. She was glad as well, she too was hungry.

Shameka didn't bother to look up and continued to mull over the menu. She wasn't a huge fan of Naomi but she still tried to be polite to her sisters' friend. To her she was bourgeois and unauthentic.

"Hey boo!" Naomi said, greeting Shaleea. "Hey Shameka!"

"Hey girl," Shaleea responded to her friend while quietly shaking her head at her sister who hadn't bothered to respond. Naomi took off her coat and took a seat.

"So how you been, I haven't seen you in forever." Naomi didn't seem to mind the blatant disregard from Shameka. She was used to it.

"I been busy with home and class. The businesses have been hectic also. A pipe burst a week ago and it was water everywhere. We had to close down for a few days. It cost a grip to fix."

"Damnnn. That's crazy. It has been cold as fuck tho. I know that shit was hectic."

"Definitely. Noah cried like a baby when they told him how much it was going to be to fix it," Shaleea laughed.

"Noah so goddamn cheap," Shameka chimed in. She liked Noah and knew of his notorious penny-pinching ways.

"Yesssss honey. But will spend hundreds of dollars per month on his smoke. He kills me with that shit. But that's my boo tho."

"Yeah now...He wasn't a month ago," Shameka laughed.

"Whatever hoe, mind ya business," Shaleea replied. It had only been a month since her and Noah had gotten back together, but she was for the most part happy.

"So what's up with ya boy Mann. I tried to call him but he don't even be responding," Naomi asked.

Shaleea grew uncomfortable at the mere mention of Mann. She hadn't seen Mann in almost a month. She didn't want to flat out tell Noah that she didn't want him at the house since he would question her about why. They conducted business and Mann was his friend so Noah wouldn't understand her reasoning if she stated such. Instead she told him she wanted them to work on getting their house back to a home and preferred to stay private for a while. Noah still brought him by once but she stayed in the room and pretended to be sleep.

"Girl that's Noah's boy, not mine," she said with clarity. "And I don't know what's up with him...Mann is weird sometimes." She knew why he wasn't answering his phone, he was too busy sporadically calling her instead. He made it very clear with his voicemails and text messages that he was interested in Shaleea.

"Yeah he does act odd," Naomi agreed. "I think he likes you," she said bluntly, surprising Shaleea. She looked to Shaleea and waited for a response to her "out of the blue" statement.

"What?" Shaleea said with a cough. The Pepsi she was drinking caused her to choke a little when Naomi made the statement.

"Naaa, I don't think so...What happened to the dude you was talking to that you told me you met in Jollies?" Shaleea asked, referring to a popular bar in North Philly. She wanted to change the subject. She figured now wasn't the time but she would eventually have to tell Naomi that Mann did in fact like her. She wasn't quite sure when that would be though.

"Girl nothing. He was mess, a straight user...A lot of these dudes are. Times have changed and a lot of these niggas be trying to live off females. The shit is sad."

"They definitely do, but it depends on how you carry yaself that determines what type of men

DECEIT, LIES, AND ALIBIS 2

you attract," Shameka said, butting in again. The statement seemed kind of rude to Shaleea and she wanted to get off the subject of men completely.

Shameka always thought Naomi was a weak bitch that faked her confidence so she wouldn't be transparent enough for people to see through. Naomi just seemed thirsty to her. Not only thirsty, but desperate and shady. Surprisingly, she was extremely pretty but she was overweight. Although she seemed to carry it well, Shameka was sure it still posed as a problem as well as an insecurity for Naomi when it came to meeting men. She was surprised Shaleea couldn't pick up on it. In all actuality Shaleea did but would never speak on it. She would let Naomi talk about it when she felt comfortable to do so.

"There's our food," Shaleea stated. She was glad they could eat and put an end to the conversation.

Shaleea and Shameka walked through Michael's Arts and Craft Store looking for decorations for Gina's upcoming birthday party. It was the middle of January and her birthday was in a few weeks.

"These are cute. We can make some nice glass centerpieces," Shameka said, picking up a nice but affordable "do it yourself" set.

"Yeah they are nice, get nine of them. The room we renting has ten tables. The main table, the one Mommy's going to be at is going to be set up differently."

"Ok. Let me ask you a question Leea." Shameka said inquisitively.

"Why you look like that when Naomi started talking about Noah's friend?"

"Who Mann?" Shaleea asked, playing dumb.

"Bitch you know who I'm talking about?" she laughed.

"I ain't look no type of way…Naomi likes him but honestly he's not interested in her like that. Naomi is kind of aggressive with guys though and I don't want to hurt her feelings by telling her she needs to tone it down a little," Shaleea confessed.

"Which one is Mann anyway….I remember Hakim, the one that passed away. I don't think I met Mann."

"Umm, he got a bald head, kind of dark

skinned. Hood ass nigga that got a black Dodge Charger."

"Ohhhh ok. I met him at the house. He was outside talking to Noah when I dropped off Heaven…He fine as hell."

"Yeah he aight," Shaleea said, once again wanting to end the conversation. She wasn't sure why Shameka brought him up.

"Does he really like you like Naomi said?"

Shaleea laughed. Her nosey ass sister was so persistent. "Yeah he do…But—"she began, before Shameka cut her off.

"Uh huh. I knew you looked like that for a reason. He is fine as shit, I'd piss all on that bald head if he asked," she laughed.

"Would you shut the fuck upppp!" Shaleea said, laughing hysterically. "You say anything."

"I say what a bitch *want* to say, but *won't*. Let me find out you want to give Mann some cookies and milk…or have already…" she suggested, staring at Shaleea with her eyebrow raised.

"Girl bye! I'm going to the car. You paying."

"Yeah alright bitch. Those tables will be bald as Mann's head," she joked, before the two walked up to the sales counter to pay for their items.

FOUR

Noah

Noah fumbled with his keys as he struggled to get his front door open. It was bitterly cold and Mann was standing behind him blowing onto his hands, while rubbing them together vigorously for warmth.

Once entering the house they hung up their coats and took a seat in the den. Shaleea suddenly appeared from the back room ready to greet Noah but stopped abruptly when she saw he wasn't alone.

"Shit," she said aloud, when she saw Mann staring at her. She hated when Noah just popped up at the house with company. And she had already told him she preferred some alone time around the house.

"Yoooo, go put some fuckin clothes on, we got company," Noah said once Shaleea came out. He walked out of the room to follow her, attempting to block what she had on display. Mann had already saw her and made no attempt to redirect his gaze when she came out. Noah didn't see it but Shaleea definitely did.

"I don't know what you snapping for. I told ya ass I didn't want a whole bunch of company. I can't walk around my own damn house cuz you got his bald headed ass here," she said.

Noah laughed lightly. "We got some business to handle, and besides it's three in the afternoon and you got ya whole fucking big black ass hanging out, Besides, I thought you was cool with Mann," he asked jokingly.

She had on some boy shorts that clung to the middle of her ass. The rest of her backside was exposed. She threw some sweatpants over the shorts and didn't bother to change her half-shirt.

"How long yall gon be?" she asked, irritated and ignoring the question he asked. She didn't want Mann's wierdo ass hanging around all day.

It was awkward and he wasn't making it any better staring at her.

"I don't know. We got some shit to handle," he responded.

"Well wrap it up Noah, I want it to just be us, and I want to be able to walk around,--- with my ass hanging out, especially since my name is on the damn deed," she reminded him.

"Yeah, well pay the mortgage then," he said sarcastically.

"Yeah ok smartass. You do payroll, use QuickBooks, and write a business plan. When you learn to do that then I'll be happy to switch places with you and just pay the mortgage," she said with a satisfied smile.

"You stay talking shit," he laughed. "You got me though, I'll take care of the mortgage…And I got sumn for that smart mouth later," he added, before walking out. She laughed to herself and shook her head.

Noah headed back out to do business with his soon to be former friend.

Shaleea

The following day Shaleea sat on the floor of the bathroom and read the plastic stick she was holding for the second time. She had taken two tests and this one said the same thing; POSITIVE. She was definitely pregnant.

After eating her normal light breakfast Shaleea didn't feel so well. Nausea and dizziness invaded her body shortly after consuming the small meal. She hadn't missed a period but she had been experiencing bouts of tiredness over the past week and decided to confirm her suspicions.

Shaleea was happy that the surgery she had months back had been successful, but she was now faced with a new problem. She wasn't sure if this baby was Noah's. She didn't remember a whole lot from the night she slept with Mann, but she did know they had went several rounds. She was sure Mann didn't use protection and she cursed herself for not being smart, or responsible enough to get emergency contraception after the encounter.

She didn't plan to say anything about the pregnancy until after she met with Dr. Davis. She had already called him and he told her to come in that week. He would confirm she was pregnant and then would perform an intravaginal ultrasound to determine how far along she was. She prayed she wasn't too far in the pregnancy. She and Noah had recently become intimate again and if it was his, she wouldn't be any more than around six weeks pregnant. Anything past that would make the baby Mann's. She took a deep breath and hoped for the best, before she got up to continue with her day.

Shaleea turned off the engine and took out the keys of the new truck Noah had purchased her. Even though she wasn't initially impressed with the truck, she still accepted it once she moved back in. The Audi was gorgeous inside and out, and she loved every bit of it.

After moving back into their home, life went back to normal for the three and Shaleea had been busier than ever. She was almost to the end of her Master's degree program and was about to begin her practicum, which was basically several semesters of her applying all that she had learned from graduate school in a practical business setting. She was having trouble coming up with ideas about ways to apply what she had learned to her business.

Since she knew she wouldn't be able to fully juggle her coursework and conduct business she and Noah decided that they would promote Susan and hire another full time attendant to cover her shift. Susan would officially become area manager for the four North Philadelphia laundromats and receive double the pay. They would pay an extra $3,200 per month overall but it didn't matter. Shaleea had to focus on finishing her degree so she could be good for the long haul. Besides they had more than enough income coming in and after being apart from Noah for several months, she realized even more how important it is to be independent.

Noah had been really sweet to her since she had moved back in. Shaleea guessed that once he got a taste of life without her, he straightened up. She knew he loved her but she sometimes didn't know if that love alone was enough to keep him on the right track. He did however, make some changes, starting with changing his phone number and committing to being home every night by nine. She prayed they made it. Lord knows she loved him.

"Hey Susan," Shaleea said to her top employee when she walked into the office of Squeaky Clean 4 at 21st and Lehigh. That was their largest laundromat and where they had their main office that they handled all of the paperwork.

"Hey Shaleea, how are you?" Susan asked. Susan was an older, short plump Puerto Rican lady who she had known for many years. She met Susan when she opened her first laundromat. She knew she would need help when she first opened up and wanted to reach out into the poor community to give someone a job. She walked into the welfare office workforce center off Lehigh and saw Susan diligently searching for jobs.

She hired her on the spot to work the overnight shift since Noah refused to do it and wouldn't allow Shaleea to do it herself. She was an awesome employee and an incredible asset to Squeaky Clean. She and Noah both adored Susan.

"Hey Susie Q, how's it going?" she asked.

"Laid back really. I had to put a few people out who were loitering and stealing muffins and coffee."

"Ohh you mean the homeless guys?" Shaleea asked.

"Yes, unfortunately I do."

"Ok. Well we definitely can't have them standing around, but next time go ahead and let them grab whatever's up there. I don't want to turn them away if they're hungry. After that they do have to move out the front," Shaleea stated, while going over an inventory sheet.

"Okey dok boss lady…Oh! I forgot to tell you someone came by here for you today." She snapped her finger profusely trying to remember what he said his name was.

"What did he look like?" Shaleea asked, after Susan failed to remember after a few seconds.

"Oh, umm he was kinda tall…well taller than me…dark-skinned, bald head—drove a black sporty looking car. "

"Oh ok, Susan. I know who it is…Thanks," she grumbled. She knew it was Mann and she was pissed that he brought his black ass up to her and Noah's laundromat. She hadn't seen him in over a month before yesterday, and he still was tripping over what happened.

"Oh yeah, he left his number. I put it on your desk."

"Ok, I'll grab it. Thanks Susan."

She was going to rip the number up as soon as she got the opportunity. Besides, she already knew Mann's number. She had called him and Hakim both on multiple occasions when she couldn't reach Noah. She wondered why he felt the need to show up at her place of business looking for her when Noah could have been present. He was up to something. She just didn't know what.

FIVE

Mann

Mann walked into his home carrying a noisy plastic bag that held soup and tea. He had drove all the way into Philadelphia to get the items and hoped his grandmother would be able to hold it down on her weak stomach.

Mann closed his door but didn't bother to lock it since the neighborhood was extremely safe. He didn't even own a security system yet. However, he planned to get one as soon as he returned from New York in a few days.

"Hey Grandma," he said with a smile. Mann's grandmother Darlene was laying in her queen sized bed watching Goodtimes. It was one of her favorite shows so Mann went and found her several seasons on Blue Ray.

"Hey baby," Darlene responded with a profound cough. The cough sounded like it came from the deep pits of her soul and actually caused her body to shake.

"You okay?" he asked, face full of concern. She had been sick for several weeks and her health was deteriorating because of her age. In just a couple of weeks she had been to the hospital several times. It pained him to see her in the condition she was in, and lately he had been thinking about how he would carry on his life without her. She and Zeke were pretty much the closest things he had to him. Zeke's mom had too died from drug abuse along with his own mother. The rest of Darlene's family were living their life and were too selfish to occasionally reach out and check on their elderly relative. For that reason Mann didn't acknowledge them. It was as if they never existed.

"I'm okay Manny, just a little under the weather baby," she hoarsely replied, calling him what she had called him for years. Everyone called him Mann, which was a nickname derived from his given name Damon, but Darlene called him Manny.

"Well, I got you some soup and the tea you like from 4th street...Where's Sonya?" he asked. He was referring to Darlene's caregiver who he had hired when they moved into the home. Darlene didn't need around the clock care but he paid Sonya to be there from 7am-3p. She would help Darlene bathe, get dressed, take her medications, and would also prepare all her meals for the day. The remainder of the day Darlene would watch T.V and sometimes Mann would drive her into Philadelphia to see some of her elderly friends or play bingo. At one point she had been fond of the slot machines at the Sugar House Casino but once her health began to fail her, she stopped going. Mann was secretly happy since she could easily go in there and waste hundreds of dollars. He wasn't into fucking up his money but he didn't like telling her no since she cared for him since he was a baby.

Both he and Zeke's moms were fast girls living in a big city. They partied, had loads of fun and tried different drugs. When crack hit the scene in the 80's, their young lives were cheated the chance to blossom properly because the drug ravaged through the community and devastated families. Mann's mother was killed when he was twelve. She had been found alongside of the Schuylkill River in West Philadelphia. The cops ruled it most likely drug related. To them she was just another dead crack-head. Zeke's mother eventually ended up falling in love with Heroin when crack was no longer good enough for her. She would eventually succumb to an overdose. Darlene raised the two side by side the best she could, and loved them as well as she knew how. His grandmother was his life, as well as his hero.

"I told her she could go get some lunch. She had taken care of everything for me and I could tell she was hungry," she said, responding to Mann's earlier question. She was smiling. As long as he could remember she always had a smile on her face, even when things were bad.

"Oh that's cool. Well look Grandma, I have some business to handle. I'm gonna leave your soup by your bed in case you want some before Sonya gets back. There's a spoon and straw in the bag."

He walked over and gave her a kiss on her

thin brown cheek and left for his own room. He had to call Zeke. The "come up" day as Mann liked to call it, was swiftly approaching and he wanted to make sure he and Zeke were on the same page since the plans had changed up a little. There was no room for error.

After speaking with Zeke, Mann went to the bathroom and rummaged around his medicine cabinet. He was looking for the Tylenol he had purchased the other day. Lately he had been having a series of painful headaches and he needed something to alleviate the pain. As a child he was diagnosed with depression and anxiety that stemmed from him feeling abandoned by his mother. He remembered having the same terrible headaches then. When his mother died it was an extremely traumatic experience for him, especially because of his fragile mental state. He was too young to understand that she was sick and because of this he always felt like he was an inadequate child, incapable of being able to get something that should be a given in life; the love of one's mother. She had already chosen drugs over him and when she died that solidified that her love with drugs surpassed her love for him.

The few people he had left, he loved them fiercely and wanted to hold onto them for dear life. It was one way with Mann. He either cared for you intensely or you were in his way and he would run you the fuck over. It was that simple.

With his grandmother becoming sick, his deepest fears resurfaced. What would he do if she left him? He knew it was inevitable; she was old. He knew when the day came he would have trouble coping, so he focused on the positive. He planned to fill the void he knew would exist in his heart. Hands down Darlene was irreplaceable, but he knew Shaleea was the perfect woman to continue life with and fill the soon to be hole in his heart. He wasn't reaching her the way he wanted to currently, but eventually she would come around; once Noah was out of the picture.

Mann sat at Noah's kitchen table and the two of them counted out $25,000 for the weed they were about to cop from Dodda. Mann had convinced Noah to double their purchase from their normal twenty-five pounds weekly to fifty. Mann knew

Dodda's shipments came in monthly and he wanted to make sure he had more than what he normally would coming in. The extra hundred pounds of weed he ordered for them would be an extra hundred pounds of weed he would jack from his Jamaican mentor.

"How long you think it's gon take to move that shit?" Noah asked eagerly with an unlit Swisher dangling from his mouth.

"Well, I got my team ready for it and they usually run out completely before I pick up, so maybe a few extra days. The couple days they usually sitting with nothing, they'll be moving the extra work.

"Aight cool. That extra bread will definitely come in handy. Leea done planned this big ass party for her mom and of course I gotta foot the bill. Her ass done went and rented a big ass hall, hired a fucking comedian and gon have lions and tigers and shit roaming around," he laughed.

"Now you know you exaggerating!" Shaleea said coming out unexpectedly. She had overheard him but didn't know anyone was out there with him. She thought he was on the phone.

"Whatever," Noah laughed, before pushing

the money over to Mann so he could bag it up.

"Wassup Shaleea," Mann said, greeting her. He made intense eye contact with her and winked.

"Oh, hey Mann," she said hesitantly, growing a little nervous. Although she was extremely attracted to Mann she preferred he not be around. She really wanted to like him as Noah's friend, but it was becoming increasingly hard for her to do so. He seemed like a good guy but he was acting in poor taste by pursuing her. As intense as the night was they shared, she put it to rest in her thoughts because she loved Noah. She felt like he should do the same but he wasn't. He continued to call her and would still send numerous text messages to her phone. Additionally, he had stopped by the laundromat. She was beginning to think she had a fatal attraction on her hands or to put it plainly; the nigga wasn't wrapped too tight. To her, her and Noah's relationship was far more important than the night they shared. For as long as Mann and Noah had been friends, Shaleea assumed Mann would see it that way as well, but he wasn't. He put his energy in telling her he missed her and wanted to see her again, as well as what he could do for her.

"Well this is the first party I threw for my mom and I want to make sure she enjoys herself. It is a little pricey but nothing that's going to cripple us," she added.

"You keep saying "us." Why don't you just pay for it," he asked sarcastically.

"Noahhh, you have plenty of money and it's not like I buy bullshit. This party is for my mom. The person that feeds us well on Sundays, takes care of Heaven, anddd will most likely be providing care to your children as well...It's my mom. We're paying, and you will be happy about it," she smiled. She didn't see why he was complaining; he was going to give her what she wanted.

Mann silently disagreed with the statement she made. He didn't see the children part happening for the two of them.

"She right Noah. Give her what she want," Mann butted in jokingly.

Noah stopped and grilled Mann playfully. "Shut up nigga," he laughed. "As a matter fact, babe get the money from Mann," he suggested.

Mann smiled at Noah and then Shaleea, "Not a problem," he laughed.

Yeah, I bet, Shaleea thought, as she walked off and rolled her eyes at Mann. Out the corner of his eye, Mann watched her and admired how her form fitting sweats gripped her ass.

After loading up the cash by thousands in the duffel bag, Mann left. He was leaving for New York first thing in the morning. He hated driving through rush hour traffic but that made the transport easier. He would be able to blend right in with the average Joe. Besides tomorrow would be his final drive to the city. He had a new connect lined up in Philly and he knew that by tomorrow he would have officially worn out his welcome in the city that never sleeps.

The next morning at 7am, Mann and Zeke pulled up to the apartment building they usually met Dodda at. It was cold and large snowflakes had begun to trickle from the sky. The forecast called for six inches so they had to complete their task quickly so they could head out of the city and avoid the soon to be hazardous roadways.

Zeke slowly sipped his Arizona iced tea as he

sat beside his older cousin Mann. He listened to him repeat the same instructions for the fifth time. Zeke had heard him the first four times and wished his big cousin would have more confidence in him. He knew he had fucked up in the past, but this time would be different. There was a lot of money involved and he wouldn't let his cousin down. He hadn't smoked weed in two days and had made sure he was well rested so he would be fully focused. Zeke scratched in his scruffy braids and continued to listen. Although 25, Zeke didn't look a day over 19. Browned skinned with a baby face, he was the complete opposite of his cousin Mann, who was a dark-skinned bearded thug.

"As soon as Dodda walks out and closes the door to head to the car we count to five and will fire on our targets. Those niggas won't know what hit them. Silencer in place, head shot, we leave gun still smoking. In and out so we can catch and follow the nigga to the crib. Snatch the nigga at the door, get the bread. We kill everybody in the house. I don't give a fuck who it is. His son in school so we don't have to worry about him. Got it nigga?" Mann asked, after running down the game plan for the final time.

"I got it cuzzo," he responded.

"Good," he said, and then patted him on the back the way a proud father would his son before his first game.

Mann was excited but nervous. However, he displayed a level of calm that was almost scary. Despite the image he projected, he had a lot on his mind. His grandmother was still sick and Shaleea wasn't returning his calls; not that he expected her to. But nevertheless it was still unsettling.

"Good, let's roll," he said, before putting his thoughts aside and hopping out of the car.

The duo proceeded to make their way into the Brooklyn hi-rise that was a staple in the slums. As they made their way into the dark, piss smelling halls, a mangy gray cat scurried over Mann's feet, further rattling his nerves.

"Fuck," he murmured, before sending the cat sailing from the swift kick of his foot. Mann's actions caused Zeke to chuckle. It was only a cat. He figured he just had a lot on his mind. When they reached the door Mann proceeded to perform the custom knock Dodda requested. Three seconds later, Ty pulled the door open and allowed the two cousins to enter. He didn't bother to greet the two. He didn't care much for the young man Dodda liked so much.

Ty's dry dreads stood taller than before and appeared to be matted in the back. Mann noticed he still carried the same nine millimeter in his waist. Garlan was in his assigned spot by the door near the room Dodda sat in. However, he was heavily armed with an AR 15 assault rifle.

They walked to the back where Dodda was talking on the phone. He quickly ended his conversation when he saw Mann.

"Ok boi, I gotta go. I be dere soon to grab it," he said, before using his black hand to push the end button on his phone.

"Hey Mann boy," he smiled cheerfully. He considered Mann one of his most loyal customers.

"Wassup big homie. Everything good? Trying to get this shit and get on the road," Mann stated casually. He had not an ounce of guilt for what he was about to do.

"Yeah, everyting good. I just gotta make a run and I be back soon...Business good eh?" he asked, his dry, shoulder length dreads dangling at the sides. "You back soon and you buy much more," he smiled, his heavy Jamaican accent still prevalent.

"Yeah business is real good. Me and my patna been making some moves."

"Good. Good. Well sit down and get comfortable Mann. I be back soon," he stated before walking off. As he walked to the door Mann's heart began to race and he felt adrenaline rush through his body. Zeke looked at him for confirmation. As soon as the door slammed, Mann reached in his waist and withdrew his sound suppressed Glock 9. *One, two, three, four, five*, he counted the seconds.

"Swoop Swoop!"

The silenced gun sounded like a basketball going perfectly through the hoop. The bullet ripped through the barrel and pierced Garlan's skull. His big black body immediately crumpled to the dirty floor. A small mist of blood coated the wall along with brain matter. As soon as Ty heard the sound he wildly swung around and hit the floor, immediately reaching for his gun. He was too late, Zeke already had his drawn to quickly and quietly release two shots to Ty's chest. He struggled for breath while making eye contact with Mann. He should have checked him at the door. It was Dodda's fault. Dodda viewed Mann as family...but he wasn't. He had warned Dodda about "snake eyes." That is what he called him because he could see through the smooth talk and lies. He knew Mann was a snake; he could see it as clear as day in his eyes. Now they would pay the price for Dodda's ignorance. Ty went to speak but was silenced by the bullet Mann put through his cheek.

"I told you aim for his fuckin head," Mann snapped. "The goal is to kill." The two bodies lying in the living room floor didn't bother him one bit. He had killed before and he had no problem killing again.

The two quickly exited the apartment and took the steps to catch Dodda. As they fled the building, they saw Dodda getting in the driver side. Scared he would drive off, Mann called out to him. Mann could have waited for Dodda to return with the specified amount of drugs, but Mann wanted everything Dodda had at his home.

"Dodda," Mann called out a second time, slightly out of breath from running down the stairs.

Dodda peered back at the building and saw Mann approaching his van with Zeke. He looked at the two confused, but still waited. He became more puzzled when Mann by-passed his window and hopped in the front passenger seat of the van. Zeke was right behind him.

"What's goin on?" he asked.

Mann pulled his gun back out and aimed it at Dodda's midsection.

"Drive the fucking car to the crib. I want everything. You already know what it is," he calmly stated to his mentor.

"Mann?" he asked in the form of a question. His large poppy eyes searched Mann's for answers. Dodda was at a loss for words. He continued to search Mann's eyes for truth, and found all that he needed. He found deceit and years full of lies. He had grown to care for Mann like a son. He should had never trusted him enough to let him enter the side house without being searched. He glanced up to the apartment and knew his cousins were dead.

Mann wiped the sweat away from his bald head while he kept his other gloved hand tightly gripped around his Glock. Zeke said nothing. He was merely a sidekick, there for added muscle.

"Dere's nothing at da house but my family. I was on my way to pick up," he stated. There was no way in hell he was taking them to his house with his wife and son. He would readily die first.

Mann grinned and looked back at Zeke. He had hit the fucking jackpot. Instead of weed, Dodda had cold hard cash.

"Where is it?" Mann asked, with the gun still pointed, and a cold smile still stretching across his face.

"It's in da side panel attached to da door."

Dodda didn't bother to question Mann about why he was doing what he was doing. He was disappointed since he had shown nothing but love to the young nigga since he met him in the penitentiary. What attracted him to Mann was the hunger in his eyes; his passion. Ironically that is what he would use to betray him with. Mann was hungry for money and Dodda had plenty. He knew better than to put so much trust into Mann. He had nothing when he met him, not even the basic necessities such as commissary. He remembered feeding the youngster on numerous occasions. Although saddened by his betrayal,

Dodda too had his own reasons for keeping the much younger Mann around.

While locked away age eventually began to overcome him. While the time on Earth made him wiser, it was like his kryptonite, making him weaker. He was no longer able to physically defend himself the way he used to. Mann served as his protector. He had a violent reputation in the prison and that alone was enough to keep Dodda from the deadly grasp of the wolves behind the prison walls. Dodda should have known this day was inevitable. He had led himself to foolishly believe something other. There was no such thing as loyalty anymore in these cold streets.

As Zeke ripped off the side paneling of the back door of Dodda's Toyota Sienna, Mann's eyes lit up like the lights on a Christmas tree. The bundles of cash were neatly counted and taped to the inside of the door.

"Check the other one," he instructed Zeke. He knew there was more. Once Zeke ripped open the other side, he saw more neatly stacked bundles. It was $600,000 in all. Enough for 2,000 pounds of weed; his monthly shipment.

Dodda's eyes frantically darted around the

parking lot searching for a way to escape. Bullets were the norm in that section of Brownsville. He wasn't worried about the money, he had plenty at his home. What worried him was that Mann's eyes displayed a bitter coldness. He knew he planned to kill him. Besides, he knew the old saying well, *"If they're masked up they're coming for your ice. If they're bare faced they're coming for your life."* Neither of the two attempted to conceal their faces. He regretted having the dark tint applied to the windows of the van. Mann laughed hysterically at the sight of all the money.

"What you want me to put it in?" Zeke asked Mann. They had come thinking they would be snatching duffel bags of weed. They had nowhere to put the money. Mann thought for a second and then began pulling off his jacket to load the cash. While he did that, he foolishly placed the gun in the center of his lap. Seizing the opportunity, Dodda grabbed for the gun, cocked it and immediately fired.

The bullet from the Glock shattered the window and missed Mann's head by a mere inch. Dodda continued to fire wildly in the car as Mann fought for dear life to get the gun out of his hands.

He quickly overpowered the older man with the help of his cousin.

As soon as Mann got ahold of the weapon, he fired three shots into Dodda's chest, killing him nearly instantly.

"Fuck ass nigga," he yelled, shaken by the fact that Dodda had almost bodied him. "Zeke get the money," he firmly stated, while wiping Dodda's splattered blood away from his face. They had to get the fuck outta dodge. It was broad daylight and the cops would eventually show up.

"Zeke, you hear me," he asked again, as he continued to wipe at his eyes. Zeke didn't respond.

Mann turned around to speak to his cousin, but lost his breath when he saw Zeke was slumped over the seat with a hole through the front of his head.

"Fuck, fuck, fuck!" Mann yelled hysterically in the van, as he punched on the dashboard. The sight of his dead cousin was enough to bring him to his knees. Mann sobbed deeply, his chest heaving up and down. However, no tears fell. The pain was deeper than that. It was his fault; he got his cousin killed. He looked back at his cousin and knew what he would have to do. He would have to leave him. Mann threw his hoodie over his head and hopped out of the car. The snow was coming down much heavier and was turning the area into what appeared to be a winter wonderland. However, he knew that it was no wonderland. It was nothing more than a white, snow covered jungle.

After he retrieved all the money from the door panels, he quickly walked to where his rented van was parked and loaded up the cash.

He opened the trunk and searched for the spare gas container the rental company provided. He was happy to see there was still gas in it. He felt in his pocket for his lighter and carefully headed back to the car, looking around to make sure no one saw him. After opening the door, Mann quickly doused Dodda with the gas. He snatched a loose bill from his pocket and lit it, before throwing it on Dodda's dead body and running back to his van. The fire ripped through the van, burning every piece of evidence and fingerprint in it. It also destroyed what was left of his cousin Zeke.

SIX

Shaleea

Shaleea walked out of Dr. Davis's office around 10am with a seemingly permanent smile covering her face. She was excited. Her doctor had confirmed she was indeed pregnant and estimated her to be around five weeks. It was Noah's baby and she couldn't wait to tell him. Her last pregnancy she had only carried for two months before finding out the baby was in her tube, but this time her doctor did an ultrasound and confirmed the baby was attached to the uterus.

She already knew exactly how she would tell him and Heaven. This was a big moment and she planned to tell them together. She didn't care if it was a boy or a girl; she was just thankful.

Shaleea was also happy that Mann should definitely get the picture now that she was pregnant by Noah. Life was almost perfect. Now she could get an understanding with Mann so he would stop the games. Sadly nothing ever goes according to plans.

Eve

Eve looked out the window of the city bus and took in the beauty outside of it. The earth in front of her was covered in a thick blanket of snow at least five inches high. Although the weather made traveling difficult, Eve still braved it in search of her baby's father. For the past several months, a few times a week she would spend half the day traveling to each of Noah's laundromats in search of him. So far she hadn't run into him but she truly believed that she would eventually.

Eve looked down at her stomach. She was now three months pregnant. Even though she wasn't very far she was already starting to show. This was becoming a problem since her body was her bread and butter. The further along she advanced in her pregnancy, the more she realized how important it was for her to find Noah. As she looked in the lightly occupied, snow covered parking lot, she smiled. Today was her lucky day.

Noah

Noah spotted Eve as she speed walked to his car. He noticed she had a pocket knife in her hand as he quickly raced to her with his fist balled up at his sides. He already knew what she was about to try to do.

"Yo what the fuck are you doing up here?" he asked with a growl. He couldn't yell like he wanted since Shaleea was nearby inside the back office talking to Susan and reviewing some paperwork. They had planned to leave any minute and Shaleea was going to be walking out very soon. He had to get Eve out of sight fast.

"You've been ignoring my fucking calls and trying to flee me like I'm a bum bitch. All you give a fuck about is that hoe in there," she said, pointing to the building.

"How she gon feel when I tell her I'm three

months pregnant with your child... Huh dickhead?!" she asked. "You woulda known that if you hadn't been ignoring me and then changed your number." She folded her knife and safely placed it back in her pocket. She was glad she was able to quietly get his attention.

Noah stood outside at a loss for words when she made her revelation. *Fuck!* he yelled internally. The last thing he needed was for Eve's ass to go to Shaleea and lie about being pregnant by him. Things were going good between them and there was no way on God's green earth that he would let her fuck that up again.

Pulling her by her arm, Noah pulled her closely to him. They were now nose to nose.

"Bitch if you are fuckin pregnant it's not mine. And don't you fucking even think of stepping to my girl with that nut shit. I promise you won't get the results you're looking for," he snarled threateningly. He no longer had a use for Eve and he had no time to play games with her. She had caused enough problems.

"Don't flatter yourself nigga. I don't have to lie on you. The last time we met up in December you were drunk. We fucked raw dumb ass. It's ya baby....I will have it and you will take care of both of us, or you can kiss your relationship with that black ass bitch goodbye," she snarled, while making a bye gesture with her fingers. Just as he was about to respond Susan walked out of the laundromat.

"He's outside Shaleea," she stated by the door, after seeing Noah standing at the car. Shaleea wasn't too far behind her following her out. She had been looking for him so they could leave.

In a panic, Noah reached in his pocket and hit the unlock button on his key fob. "Get the fuck in the truck before she see you," he whispered with anger.

Rolling her eyes, Eve slowly got in Noah's Range Rover. The windows were darkly tinted so Shaleea couldn't see inside. Luckily for Noah she didn't see Eve but he wasn't sure if Susan did or not.

"Hey babe, what you doing outside in the cold?" she asked, before leaning in to give him a kiss. Seeing the two of them made Eve want to cry. She wished Noah would love her like he loved Shaleea. He made it very clear he didn't.

"I had to make a phone call and the machines

were loud...Listen I gotta handle some shit at the truck. Truck manager just called and said it's two employees over there bout to get it on. I'm gon run over and talk to them real quick. I'll be home after okay...You want me to bring you anything?" he asked, hoping she would hurry up so he could dump Eve off somewhere.

"No I'm okay, but what time are you going to be back in. Heaven is having her chorus concert this evening at six. That's just a few hours...Everyone is going to be there to see her sing and she's expecting you there as well."

"I'm just gonna handle this real quick and I'll meet you at the house. Tell Heaven don't worry. I'll be there," he smiled.

"Ok," she said, before giving him a kiss and walking off to her own car. He was happy they had driven separate cars that day. The sight in front of her made Eve sick. She was tempted to hop out and cause a scene. Once Shaleea walked off Noah quickly got in the car and prepared to deal with Eve's ass.

After turning on the car, Noah quickly pulled off out of the parking lot. He didn't feel secure knowing Shaleea was so close by. After driving for a few minutes and making sure Shaleea didn't follow him, he let his fury spill out.

"Yo what the fuck is wrong with you?!" he asked, looking at Eve like she had lost her mind. The anger caused lines to appear on his forehead and sweat to form on his nose.

"I already told you why I had to come up here. I'm already starting to show and I can't make any money dancing," she stated, with the half-truth. "I need security Noah…A house, a car, stuff for the baby…I need *you*."

"Are you stupid or something?" he asked her. "Can you not hear? You can't keep that baby. If what you say is true and it is mine, you can't keep it. I have my own situation. I have a fucking family…I already have a kid on the way by my girl," he revealed.

After Shaleea came from the doctor's office she went to Hallmark and got a gift box to wrap up her pregnancy test and sonogram. She presented it to Noah and Heaven as soon as Heaven got out of school. Noah was elated and it angered him that Eve was coming to him with the bullshit and most likely lies.

"So I'm good enough to fuck, but I ain't good

enough to have your baby!?" Eve questioned, immediately growing upset.

"You want me to kill my baby but that bitch can keep hers?" she asked. "You have more than enough money to take care of our baby too!" This was not how the situation was supposed to go.

"Eve...I love her. I have a family. Whatever we have is over. I'm gon try to do right by her...them. As fucked up as it sounds, you can't have that baby. You gotta get rid of it. I'll give you whatever you need to make that happen, and I'll throw in some extra to help you get on ya feet after...But you can't keep it...." he stated firmly, watching the tears well up in her eyes.

"For what it's worth, I'm sorry for what I put you through, but...I gotta do what's right from this point on," he revealed sincerely.

He knew what role he played in the months' worth of drama, but Eve had truly brought it on herself when she played like a child in a grown-up game.

Although what Noah was saying made sense to him, to Eve, what he was saying was nothing more than selfish inaudible words that she couldn't make out. They sat in silence the remainder of the ride, except for Eve telling him where to drop her off. When she finally exited the car Noah gave her his number and told her to contact him when she set up the appointment. He wanted to be with her when it all happened. Even though he wasn't sure if the baby was his or not, he couldn't risk taking the chance and not handling the problem.

She took the number and walked off, crying silent tears. Her pain would soon be shared. She had no intention of calling him. She was having their baby. She had just been struck with an ugly dose of reality. Noah didn't give a fuck about her and never ever would. Even though he had shown that numerous times before, today was the day he stamped and sealed that confirmation.

Eve took the torn piece of paper with the number and ripped it to pieces before tossing it to the ground. She reached in her coat and pulled out another piece of paper. This one was more important. It was Noah's registration to his truck. She had taken it out of his glove box when he was standing outside talking to Shaleea. She had learned three things that day: one, Noah didn't give a fuck about her, two, Noah's new phone number, and three, his permanent address that was listed on the registration. That was all she needed.

SEVEN

Noah

Noah sat on the king size bed curled up next to Shaleea and Heaven. It was Saturday and they were all sitting around watching some old episodes of Shaleea's favorite zombie show. He reached over to Shaleea and rubbed her belly. He had been spending a lot more time home lately ever since finding out she was pregnant. He was so excited he was about to become a dad. Although he loved Heaven like she was his own, he knew nothing would compare to watching his own child come into the world. It would be epic.

While watching the show he heard his phone chirp. He suspected it was Mann responding since he had been calling and texting him repeatedly to see how he was doing. When he returned from his trip to New York he was acting really strange and distant. After a little probing Mann confessed that his grandmother had fallen ill over the course of several days and was in the hospital. Noah even went to visit her to support his friend. He was shocked to see her gravely skinny and hooked to oxygen.

After looking down at his phone he realized it wasn't Mann. It was Eve texting him. His heart skipped a beat in his chest when he read the message.

Come outside

"Who's that?" Shaleea asked from the bed. She was perched up on one arm, curled against Heaven still watching TV.

"It's Mann…he stressing. I'ma go and call him back in the living room," he lied.

Once he closed the door to the bedroom, he raced to the front of the home to see if Eve really had the balls to show up to his house. After peering out the window, he realized her ass had balls the size of Texas. Eve and Bianca stood stone-faced in the front of his home like they lived there.

Luckily for him the alarm wasn't set, and he quietly opened the door to see what the two bitches wanted. His hands twitched at his sides. He had to quickly calm himself since he really wanted to knock them both out.

"Yo are you fucking crazy," he whispered. "Get the fuck away from my house!"

"I'm not going anywhere Noah! And I suggest you show me and my friend some respect before I cause a scene up in dis funky ass neighborhood of yours," Eve snarled while swinging her platinum blond weave.

"I just come to tell you I ain't getting an abortion. I want $5,000 and the same amount every month from dis point on." She knew he had it since he was out in his wealthy ass neighborhood pretending to be the fucking Huxtables.

Eve was tired of playing games with Noah. If she couldn't have his heart, she would get the next best thing; some of his money. She was tired of living in a dingy hotel room, catching the bus, while he went home every night to what looked like a million dollar townhouse.

"Bitch I'm not giving you no fuckin $5,000 every month!" he snarled, ready to pounce on the two. He made his way to them causing them to step back.

He was losing his patience. They wanted to act like niggas by approaching him so he was about to treat them like niggas. He thought about just telling Shaleea the truth but he didn't know how she would react. Knowing Shaleea, she would force him to take a paternity test. He couldn't risk it. If the baby ended up being his, he knew it would be over for good.

"You betta back the fuck up," Eve threatened, gripping her mace tightly.

"Look, get away from my fucking house. I'll have the money tomorrow," he agreed with an angry sigh. He didn't have a choice at the moment. Shaleea could walk out any minute. He was going to have to figure out a way to get a grip on the situation with Eve. Not only was she a headache, but she was truly fucking his life up.

Eve looked to Bianca and smiled in satisfaction. It had actually been Bianca's idea to pop up demanding money. Noah was selfish and it was her turn to be a real live dickhead. She was far from finished; she was just getting started.

Noah watched the pair walk off to the Germantown Cab that was parked quietly up the street. *Fuckin birds*, he silently thought. Closing the door he walked back into the house. Once he got back in the room he was happy to see that Shaleea and Heaven had fallen asleep. He didn't feel like making up any more lies; he was tired of lying.

Noah pulled out his iPhone to dial Mann again. After seven rings the voicemail picked up. He wanted to see how he was doing but he too also needed someone to confide in. It was hard being there for Mann when he just closed himself off out of the blue. He wasn't returning call or text messages and he hadn't been conducting business either.

Noah decided he would go check on Mann tomorrow. His new house wasn't too far away and he wanted to make sure he was holding up okay. That was the least he could do. Besides, the fresh air and drive would give him some time to figure out what to do about Eve.

Mann

Mann blinked his eyes several times and realized he had nodded off. He had been at the hospital all morning and not much had changed. He took his grandmothers hand and rubbed it in his. She was lying peacefully in the small makeshift bed. He prayed she would be okay. He leaned back in the multicolored hospital chair and sighed. His head was pounding from stress.

Ms. Darlene had been asking about Zeke all morning and he was distraught with guilt. She couldn't understand why Zeke hadn't been there to see her when she had been in the hospital for a week. There wasn't a day that passed that she didn't ask Mann to go search for him. She expressed her concern and although Mann knew the truth, he pretended to worry along with her, when in reality heavy grief consumed him.

"Manny baby, why don't you go on home and get some rest," she stated hoarsely. It was after nine at night and Mann had been there since visiting hours started at seven.

"I'm okay Grandma, just get some rest," he responded while scratching his beard.

"Manny, I'm not asking you. I'm telling you.

Go home, wash up and get some rest baby. You been up here all day," she said with a cough. "I'll be fine. Besides I'm a little tired and I'm going to rest my eyes."

After some hesitation, Mann finally agreed. He went home, took a shower and did his best to get some rest. However, the severe headaches he suffered from, as well as grief from Zeke and worry over his grandmother caused him to lie wide awake. He refused to smoke since the THC in the marijuana put him in deep, trance like thoughts. He eventually pulled out an old bottle of E&J from the fridge and threw the whole thing back. Liquor couldn't take away the pain but it damn sure could suppress it.

That night would be the last night Ms. Darlene spent in the hospital. In the early morning hours she would pass away in her sleep. The pain Mann felt was unspeakable. He had no one and he was empty. His mind state was extremely fragile and the headaches became unbearable. To function he kept alcohol and pain killers in his system. It wasn't enough however, to stop the storm brewing from within his body.

Noah made himself comfortable in the living room of Mann's home the following day. He had come by as planned to check on his dear friend, and was saddened by what he saw. Mann was sitting by the window drinking, eyes red from crying from the loss of his grandmother. As tough as Mann appeared to be on the exterior, Noah knew that he was hurting inside.

"I know that shit hurts my nigga but you will get through it," Noah stated, attempting to offer Mann some kind words. He figured he wouldn't stay long since he probably wanted to be alone. "If you need anything, say the word and I got you," Noah offered.

"Nah I'm good, I got bread," Mann responded, almost defensively. He didn't want shit from Noah, nor did he need shit from Noah. Once he came up on the $600,000 Mann no longer wanted to be bothered with him. He had one final use for Noah and then he would be done with him completely.

"Oh I got that bread for you too," he stated, before getting up off the leather recliner and heading to his master suite to retrieve Noah's $8,750. That was his 35% of the fifty pounds of weed sold for the week. Although Mann had barely sold any of the weed he wanted to pay Noah off. Their business dealings were over.

"I'm gonna fall completely off the weed shit. I'm gon focus on burying my Grandma," Mann said lying, before sitting back down in the recliner.

Noah took the money and didn't bother to count it. Something was off about Mann but Noah dismissed it since he was grieving. He didn't care about the dissolution of the business endeavor since he was good one way or the other. The weed investment was more of a favor to Mann. He still had income coming in from the laundromats as well as the two seafood trucks he owned with Nikka.

"That's cool. You just focus on getting yaself together," Noah stated, genuinely sincere. "Hit me up or come through the crib. Anytime you need," Noah offered, while Mann stood up to shake his hand before he left.

"Oh and I almost forgot to tell you, Leea's pregnant.

"Word?" Mann asked surprised. That had

garnered his attention. "It's yours?"

"Of course," he laughed at the insinuation. He wasn't sure where that comment stemmed from.

"I mean… yall did have that period of separation," he slyly suggested, discreetly trying to put a bug in Noah's ear. "But damn…, congratulations my nigga."

"Thanks Mann. Listen take care my nigga. Get some rest and you gon be aight Bull. Don't drink too much," he added, before walking out the door.

Mann watched Noah walk off and went back in his master suite to nurse his bottle. He was going to eventually contact Shaleea's ass and find out who the fuck really was about to be a father. Him or Noah?

EIGHT

Shaleea

Shaleea sat at her desk and continued to order inventory for the upcoming week. She took a deep breath and rubbed her belly. Pregnancy was such an unforgettable time but she would be glad when it was over. She was tired all the time, felt fat as fuck, and although unnoticeable to others, she could detect the presence of ugly stretch marks creeping up on her belly and thighs.

Several months had passed and she was close to five months pregnant. Lately Noah had been pressing her about them buying a larger house since he said they needed more space before the arrival of the baby. She thought there townhouse was just fine for the three of them. Nevertheless, they had just closed on a large brick house in the same development Nikka and Hakim lived. They were supposed to get the keys tomorrow.

Shaleea continued to look through the catalog, selecting products to order until the sound of knocking at her office door stopped her. She got up to open the door assuming it was Susan since Noah was watching a boxing match at a bar in North Philly.

"Hey--," she went to greet Susan, but stopped short when she saw it was Mann.

"Wassup," he asked with a slight slur. He reached his large hand out for hers, but she quickly pulled it back.

"Hey Mann, what's up, Noah's not here," she replied nervously. She could tell he had been drinking.

"I ain't looking for Noah. I came here to see you," he stated, shutting the office door.

He had waited several months to approach Shaleea about her being pregnant because he had been too busy running his growing Marijuana empire. Since he had returned from New York and cut business ties with Noah, he had been getting a lot more money. This was because he was able to buy much more from his new connect and keep all of the profits for himself.

Noah had no idea Mann was still selling weight, instead thinking that his friend had taken a hiatus because of his grandmother's death. No longer focused on longevity and a future, Mann was letting the large cash go to his head. The weed, alcohol, and pills he kept in his system didn't help him either.

"Well wassup, I was just about to leave," she stated, walking back over to her desk to grab her Chanel purse.

"Really?" he asked. "Well it's Monday and I know that's the day you come in and do paperwork. You're usually here to around 10." He looked down at his wrist to his watch. "It's 9:03."

Shaleea briefly stared at Mann. He had been following her. She was in fact usually there on Mondays until ten, and the only way Mann could have known that is if he had been following her.

"I ain't gon take up much of your time though. I only want a few minutes…I heard you were pregnant and I just wanted to see for myself, as well as determine if that's my baby you're carrying," he stated calmly, while admiring her pregnant state. Hands down she was still beautiful. Her dark chocolate skinned seemed to have a radiant glow and she carried the extra weight very well.

"I'm not sure why you would think that since we only fucked once, while we were drunk," she reminded him. "Besides, I had a very accurate sonogram from a very excellent doctor who confirmed I conceived in January, not in December," she explained.

The revelation was an immediate disappointment to Mann since he was hoping there was a possibility the baby was his.

"Does Noah know about us?" he asked, almost in a threatening manner.

"He doesn't need to know and why would he know. I'm damn sure not telling him and neither are you," she said glaring at him intensely. Throwing her bag over her arm, she prepared to walk out the door. "Look I gotta go, is that all you wanted?" she said, not really asking since she was already to the door. However, Mann stopped her.

Grabbing her by the arm he forced her into the wall and began to kiss on her neck. Shaleea's body couldn't help but respond to the kiss. However, she immediately pushed him off her.

"Yo are you crazy Mann? I'm fucking pregnant and Noah is still your friend," she firmly stated. "Why are you doing this?...Look, what happened between us in the past, and I prefer to leave it there."

"What if I don't want to?" he asked. "I want you Shaleea. I don't give a fuck about Noah. I want you...I care about you," he admitted with a wild drunken look in his eyes. The sight scared Shaleea. She had started a dirty game months back and she didn't know how to end it. She was speechless.

Mann pushed himself back onto Shaleea and rubbed his hand between her thighs while he tried to kiss her neck again.

"Mann get off me," she demanded. He continued, so she asked again. When there was no response she used all her strength to push his stocky body from up against hers.

"Get out!" she stated, while pointing to the door. He just looked at her and smiled.

"What if I don't?" he asked. "You gon call Noah," he asked mockingly. "Keep playing with

DECEIT, LIES, AND ALIBIS 2

me and I'll fuck that nigga over," he spat. "Remember you fucking started this shit back at the hotel. Besides the nigga you love is playing ya ass anyway. Why don't you ask him about that situation he got?"

"What are you talking about?" she asked, puzzled.

Although Mann and Noah were no longer doing business together they still spoke periodically. Noah had met up with him and told him about what was going on with Eve. He hadn't decided what to do about her, but for the last few months he had been religiously sending her the money she demanded. Of course, Shaleea had no idea what was going on. At this point Mann had no problems admitting how he felt. He hadn't spoken to Noah in several weeks.

"I ain't telling you anything," he stated. "You too blind to see that I really fuck with you and could do everything Noah can do. I could treat you better. You don't even see how you're really being treated," he added to get her to think. "Once you figure it out, call me."

Mann walked out, leaving Shaleea in thought about what he was talking about. Noah was hiding something. *What*, was the question? She watched Mann pull away from the laundromat in a 2015 BMW 650i. He had definitely came up on some money, and he was letting it go too far to his head.

Mann had turned into an entirely different person and she wished she could tell Noah how his supposed friend "really" felt about him. One thing for sure is that he would no longer step foot in her house again. She didn't care how Noah felt about it. Mann was a ticking time bomb ready to go off. She believed the loss of his grandmother really sent him over the edge. The problem for her was that it seemed like he wanted to take her along with him.

"Shaleea you're gonna have to tell Noah the truth," Shanita stated on the phone. Shaleea had called her as soon as Mann left. She was now on her way home.

"I don't know about that. How do I go to him and tell him I slept with is best friend?" she asked sarcastically.

"You sit him down and just tell him. You're gonna have to. It happened during a bad time for yall. One thing led to another…That crazy ass nigga is gon keep fucking with you. The crazy part is you just admitted you sexually attracted to him even after the weird shit he been doing. Why I don't know, but yall gon end up fucking again or shit is just gon get worse cuz he obviously can't take rejection," she added. "And besides, they're clearly not friends anymore. Noah told you Mann had been acting weird. Now you know why. The nigga is like a bomb ready to go off at any time. And ya simple ass don't know when the fuck that's going to be."

"True…I wonder what the fuck Noah's ass is hiding?" she asked, ignoring the fact that her rude ass sister just called her simple.

"Girl, I wouldn't even worry about it. You gotta deal with that nut Mann. Besides, he probably throwing shade and talking about a bitch Noah possibly fucking…Some shit that aint even serious. You can't be stressing Leea. At the end of the day you own businesses, have lots of money in the bank, are having a baby and just got a brand new house in a gated community. If he fucking than that bitch is dying to be like you. Noah's heart is yours."

"I hear ya," she said, unimpressed. "Thanks for listening though. I just pulled up and I'm about to head in and get some rest. I have an appointment at eight to go see what I'm having," she said, focusing on something more positive.

"Aight boo, just text me tomorrow and let me know. Be safe."

"Aight," she stated, before disconnecting the call. She looked up at her soon to be former home and sighed. What the hell had she gotten herself into?

NINE

Eve

Eve left TD Bank fuming. She had her phone to her ear and was calling Noah for the fifth time. This was her second time coming to the bank and her money wasn't there. He was supposed to have deposited the money several days ago.

She stood in front of the bank and waited for the cab she called that would take her to Chestnut Hill. She wasn't playing games with Noah. She was going to his house. He wasn't playing fair and neither was she. As she waited, her phone rang. She saw it was Noah calling back.

"Hello?" she answered on the first ring.

"Yo, you called me, wassup?" he asked. However, he already knew what she wanted.

"Noah where's my money?" she calmly asked.

"About that... I ain't giving you another dime. I gave you five Gs' for three months. That should've covered your rent for months plus brought more than enough stuff for that baby of yours," he stated.

Noah felt confident the baby wasn't his and he didn't plan to give Eve another cent. As soon as she had it, he was demanding a blood test and once it came back negative it was good riddance.

Eve immediately lost her patience. "Nigga I want my fuckin money or I'm going to ya bitch!" she yelled. She didn't care about the people around her that could overhear her ghetto tirade.

"Yeah do that and see what happens. And don't bother showing up to my house...well my old house anyway. I upgraded!" he laughed. "We in a gated community now so I can rid myself of peasant bitches like you who want to get out of line and pop up at a nigga house and shit!"

As soon as Eve showed up at his house he convinced Shaleea to start looking for another one. He used the fact that the baby was coming as an excuse of needing more space. The movers had just moved the last of the things out several days ago. Instead of the three bedroom townhouse, they now lived in a five bedroom, three story brick home. It wasn't nothing for him to drop a $30,000 down payment for them to move. They're townhouse hadn't even sold yet. As a finance major, Shaleea kept on top of the bills so well, their credit worthiness spoke volumes along with the equity in their home.

Eve hung up the phone while Noah continued to talk shit. She was pregnant and didn't have time to get herself worked up. She wasn't stressing. The baby was Noah's. As soon as she gave birth she was going to give him that blood test he had requested several times. She would let the white man at the courts force him to pay child support. Although he had sent her $15,000, she didn't have the whole thing tucked away. She still needed to live day to day and was still staying in a room. She had been trying to save up and buy a car. Instead of being modest, Eve had been looking at a small, but brand new C-class Mercedes. It was just like her to have champagne taste on a beer budget. Eve had something for

Noah's ass though. She could play with the best of them.

Noah

Noah relaxed on the plush floor of his new home. He was tired from having unpacked all day. It was a fresh start for them and he was excited. Now all he had to do was convince Shaleea to change her number. He had asked her to change it once she moved back in, but she refused since she had the number for years. He had been playing her phone super close since his encounter with Eve earlier that day. What surprised him is that she peeped it since she appeared to be watching him, watch her phone. Ironically, she had been recently secretly wishing she had changed the number as well. She was praying Mann didn't text or call her while Noah prayed Eve didn't text or call her. They both prayed internally that the phone stayed silent the remainder of the evening. She actually planned to change it in the morning.

"Bae where ya phone, I'm gon order us something to eat," he stated. He really was

DECEIT, LIES, AND ALIBIS 2

famished after unpacking all day.

"What's wrong with ya phone?" she asked, making sure she didn't sound defensive.

"It's dead. I gotta put it on the charger. It's been acting funny. Won't hold a charge long. I think I'm gon upgrade tomorrow. I can upgrade yours too if you want," he offered, hoping she took the bait so he could convince her in the store to keep the new number they gave her.

"That's cool. I did want to get that new iPhone 6," she stated. Shaleea tossed him her phone and told him what she wanted.

"Get me Shrimp Lo Mein and some fried chicken wings…Make sure you ask Heaven what she wants. She's probably not gonna want what I'm getting," she added.

"Ok," Noah replied, before taking the phone and walking up the steps. As he made his way to Heaven's room on the opposite side of the house, Shaleea's phone beeped indicating it was a new text message. He breathed a sigh of relief knowing it was probably Eve. He was glad he got the phone when he did.

Noah navigated to the text messages and saw that it wasn't Eve. It was a text message from

Mann. He immediately grew suspicious and curious as to why Mann would be contacting his girl. He read the message.

I apologize for coming at you the way I did. I just wished you would give me chance. I really care about you. That night we spent together got me in my feelings. I really dig u

Noah instantly saw red and felt like a current of emotions was traveling through him. He was more confused than anything. But if that message was what he thought it was, somebody had hell to pay. He turned away to go back to the room. His heart slammed in his chest and he felt his body fill with adrenaline. Once he reappeared in the room Shaleea knew something was wrong. He had an angry scowl painted on his normally handsome face.

"Yo what the fuck is this Leea," he asked while rapidly approaching her, jamming the phone in front of her face. His demeanor frightened her.

Shaleea quickly read the text message and lost her breath. *Fuck,* she thought. She wasn't ready to tell him but she now had little choice. No words came from her mouth when she went to speak.

"What the fuck is you deaf or something?" he asked, immediately growing angry. "What the fuck is he talking about....No let me rephrase that! Why the fuck is Mann texting you about a night yall spent together! What the fuck is he talking about?!" he yelled, grabbing her arm. He snatched the phone back and read, "*I really dig you*...What the fuck is this?!"

"Noah calm down bae...I need to talk to you." She immediately began to cry. The tables had turned and she didn't know how he was going to act when he heard the news.

"Shaleea...please tell me you not about to tell me some bullshit," he pleaded, before releasing her with a push. Her being pregnant was at the rear of his mind.

"Noah baby, just calm down please." The tears were streaming now.

"Talk!" he yelled, causing her to jump and stumble back into some boxes.

Shaleea took a deep breath and then tried to explain. "Back in December the night Naomi and I saw you at the crab truck...Well she invited Mann.

We all were drunk...At the end of the night she started throwing up. He took her home and then he was going to drop me off at my hotel...He came in to use the bathroom. One thing led to another..." she cried with her head down. "I'm so sorry Noah. I was so fucked up and so was he."

"Is that my baby," he asked with his jaws clenched. He wanted to kill them both.

"Yes. This is your son," she told him. She had just found out she was having a boy the day prior.

Noah shook his head and looked at Shaleea in disgust. Since he met her he did nothing but place her on a pedestal. She was so special to him and her betrayal was like a knife through his heart. He had never felt the way he was feeling before. Her leaving him was one thing...but this feeling was something else. His girl, his future wife, his child's mother had slept with one of his closest friends.

"So this has been going on behind my back the whole time. You two motherfuckers sat in front of me knowing yall had fucked behind my back. That's why he stopped doing business with me and started acting funny. Over ya fucking ass! I should fuck both yall up!!!" he screamed. "I'ma kill this nigga!" he threatened, feeling breathless.

He realized that everything finally made sense.

"It was a mistake Noah. It only happened once…Mann is just…"

"He's just what?! He can't get over the fact it was just a fuck! Now he want to fuck with you right!? He not used to a bitch like you!" he added disrespectfully. Shaleea was taken back by the way he spoke to her but she understood he was angry.

Feeling enraged, Noah cocked back and kicked over a lamp that lay on the floor. The broken pieces flew in the wall. He grabbed his keys off the nightstand and made his way to the front door. He had to get out of there before he did something he would regret.

"Noah please…Where are you going?" Shaleea asked. "Noah we can work through this. I'm pregnant, please don't leave me," she cried while wiping the tears away from her wet face and staring at his back.

Noah walked out of the house and didn't look back. He was going to go deal with Mann's snake ass.

◇◇◇

Noah sat in his car and slowly brought the blunt to his mouth. He pulled from it and inhaled, holding the smoke in his lungs extra-long for maximum effect. After putting the blunt out, Noah sat back in his seat and peered out his window. He was posted in front of Big Faces Bar and was hoping he spotted his ex-friend Mann. He knew there was only a handful of bars Mann frequented with this particular one being far more likely for him to be at since he used to sell the bulk of his weed in the area. He had already driven out to the county but Mann wasn't home.

After sitting in the same spot for over an hour, Noah decided to leave. Before he rolled he tried to call Mann one last time. The phone went straight to voicemail. Noah decided to leave a message.

"You already know who it is. I found out how you moving and wanted to address you on some man to man shit. Since I can't do that, I just wanted to let you know that when I see you we clutching. I never been a bitch nigga so you already know what it is. On sight nigga!"

He then hung up the phone and made his way back to his new home. He wasn't leaving Shaleea.

He loved her more than anything in the world. Besides, he knew he had put her through hell and back and it was only right that he eventually came face to face with that bitch named Karma. What she did still didn't compare to all the years of bullshit he put her through. For every action there was a reaction. Her reaction had been long overdue.

Noah couldn't help but think about negative shit as he journeyed home. He thought about how he called Shaleea numerous times the night she was with Mann. He also thought about how Mann made jokes about meeting a chick he wanted to wife. The whole time it had been Shaleea. Mann was oh so disrespectful and Noah had every intention of punching him in his mouth on site. Win or lose it was going down.

Mann

Mann listened to the voicemail twice that Noah had left him. He had to be sure that he heard what he thought he heard. Noah wanted to war with him. *Fuck clutching*, he thought. Those penitentiary days of fighting were over. If Noah came to him he better have his gun because he always kept that thang on him and he wouldn't hesitate to use it. In his mind state any nigga that came incorrectly could get it. Noah included.

Mann was getting money and had just recruited a whole new team. Fifty pounds a week with his new connect was bringing him in $40,000 a week. He felt like a boss. Bosses could have what they wanted and wouldn't tolerate any form of disrespect. That voicemail Noah left was pure disrespect and had to be dealt with.

Mann leaned over the side of his bed and dialed in the ten digits of a goon he knew in North Philly. Stick up kid turned robber, Mann knew he would knock Noah off for the right price.

"Wassup Bull," Mann asked Nootie.

"Was good my nigga," he asked Mann, who was always looking for a come up. He had known Nootie since they were kids riding bicycles on littered North Philly streets. Mann wasn't especially fond of Nootie's older brother Teddy since he was essentially a bully in the streets, always fighting somebody, moreso because he was smaller and had that little man complex. Plus

Teddy talked too much, and Mann didn't need the hot shit associated back to him. He wanted Nootie to handle this solo.

"I got a nice lil lick for you...I need you to rock sumn for me," he stated bluntly.

"Yeah...well you know that's gon cost you five," he stated calmly. It wasn't nothing for Nootie to cock his hammer back on a nigga. $5,000 to kill someone was dirt cheap and it got even cheaper when one was dealing with desperate niggas in need of fast ends.

"Cool. And I'll give you $10,000 if you do it dolo. Where you gon be, I'm gon come through in say..." He looked down at his simple, black and stainless steel Rolex to check the time, "in an hour and run down the game plan."

"I can handle that. I'll be right at Broad and Erie. My sister live right around the corner. Make sure you have half that bread with you."

"Cool see you then."

Mann terminated the call and sat back in satisfaction. Soon Noah would be out of his way. The streets talked and most of the hood knew Kiesha had set Hakim up to be robbed and killed. Both Noah and Mann knew this. Noah too had just put money on all three of their heads. Unfortunately for the two brothers, Mann never gave them fair warning. That was his warning. Since Nootie was going to be looking for Noah he would possibly have a slim chance at survival. The hit would be unlikely carried out if Noah came up missing. It was every man for himself as far as he was concerned. For now he would use the crash dummy to get Noah out of his hair.

It was no longer just about a female. Noah had disrespected him and he would see that he paid the price: with his life.

TEN

Shaleea

Shaleea had just stepped out of her Audi when she heard her phone ring. She would answer it later since she was in a hurry to sign in at her Obstetrician's office. Not too much had changed over the past couple of weeks. The baby was healthy and she was putting on the proper amount of weight. Everything seemed like it was moving so fast. School was almost over and summer too was quickly approaching. Everything was good.

After signing in at the front desk with a plump white lady, Shaleea took a seat on the large, brown leather sofa in the waiting room. She reached over to the coffee table to retrieve a copy of Jet Magazine to occupy herself until the doctor called her in. She knew it would probably be at least fifteen minutes before she went back so she made herself comfortable.

After sitting for several minutes Shaleea felt the rumbling vibration of her phone. She dug it out the bottom of her purse and saw that it was an unknown number. Without hesitation she accepted it.

"Hello," she answered.

Eve took a deep breath on the other end of the phone. "Bitch where ya man at?" she asked angrily.

Shaleea already knew who it was but she still asked, "Who is this," she whispered, so no one would hear her in the busy medical office.

"Bitch you know who it is. I'm looking for ya man…my baby daddy…oh I'm sorry…" she laughed. "*Our* baby daddy. I bet you didn't know I was six months pregnant," she taunted.

Shaleea didn't mutter a sound. She was shocked as well as instantly hurt. She had nothing to say.

"I guess da cat got ya tongue. Tell ya fuck ass

nigga I want my money!" she added to generate a response from Shaleea.

"What money?" she whispered again.

"Ya man been giving me $5,000 a month, and this month his ass is late. Tell him I want my money or he will see me *and* his daughter in court in a few months." With that said, Eve hung up the phone.

Eve already knew Noah wasn't going to give her any more money. Contacting Shaleea was merely out of spite. She knew she would really have to see Noah in court. Hopefully that was the only place she saw him. That's if she could find him.

"Shaleea Smith," a Spanish medical assistant called from the entrance to a backroom.

Hearing her name being called, Shaleea slowly stood up to head to the back. She felt a little dizzy but she proceeded anyway. She needed to have a sit down with Noah and very soon.

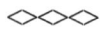

Shaleea walked out of the doctor's office knowing what she had to do. After meeting with her doctor she was told she had high blood pressure. Since she was just fine the previous visit, Shaleea concluded that it was probably stress related. With high blood pressure her baby was definitely at risk. No one was more important than Heaven and that baby that was growing in her stomach.

Dealing with Noah, Mann, school, and work was too much. She had to get away. Instead of going to Shyanne's to pick up Heaven, she went home first. When she pulled up she saw that Noah wasn't home. He had been hanging out a lot more lately after he found out she slept with his friend. She had been trying to talk to him but for the most part he had been shutting her out. She understood, he was hurt.

Shaleea looked at her beautiful new house and held back tears. She was going to have to leave it. She went in and got Heaven's favorite doll. She didn't even bother to pack a bag. She would buy what she needed. Nothing at this point was worth her sanity or the well-being of her children. She backed her car up from the paved driveway and told herself the trip was temporary; she would see her house again soon. She was headed to a peaceful place in Jersey: her fathers'.

Noah

Noah didn't fuck with many niggas especially since Hakim had died and Mann revealed he was a real live snake. So he sat in his favorite Clock Bar and made small talk with the bartender. He was on his third drink and he was definitely beginning to feel the shots of rum wreak havoc on his bladder. Holding his urine, Noah continued to think about the past day's events. Eve was still calling him with threats and he and Shaleea were barely speaking. It wasn't like she hadn't been trying to communicate with him but he was far too stubborn.

Every time he looked at her his mind created fictitious scenes of her with Mann. He wanted to move past it but he knew it was going to take some time. Noah ordered another shot of rum and got up to go take a piss outside. He didn't do nasty ass bar bathrooms.

As Noah pushed his way out of the dirty fingerprint stained glass he noticed a tall light skinned cat on the corner talking on his cellphone and a washed up fiend trying to flag down passing cars. She spoke undecipherable words to Noah but he didn't bother to turn around. The fiend who appeared to be in her late twenties, was dirty and had long been stripped of her beauty by the streets.

Noah made it to the back of the bar and unzipped his pants so he could relieve himself on a pile of old garbage. As he washed down the trash he heard a familiar sound close by; the sound of a gun cock. Noah quickly felt his waist for his burner and simultaneously spun around. It was too late to draw. He soon stood face to face with the perpetrator who was allegedly responsible for the death of his friend Hakim.

As Nootie squeezed the trigger of his firearm, Noah rushed him, crouching down low to avoid the bullet. The attack sent Nootie to the ground and Noah over top of him scrambling for the fallen gun. Noah had dressed for the warm weather so his exposed knees and elbows violently scratched the pavement as he used all his strength to grab onto the gun that was a mere few inches from him. When he reached it, he turned around and fired on Nootie, hitting him twice in the chest and killing him almost immediately.

Noah, still running off pure adrenaline immediately allowed his street instincts to kick in so he could get the fuck out of dodge. He had no time to panic unless he wanted to find himself locked away for the rest of his life. He tucked the firearm used to kill Nootie in his waistband and did his best to exit the back of the building and blend in with the pedestrians traveling the busy street. He was nervous as fuck, with sweat dripping down his beard covered face.

When he reached his car he immediately started his truck and headed back to his home. It was a close call; Nootie had truly caught him slipping. However, it wasn't hard since he always played the same bars. He prayed the cameras in the vicinity didn't catch what happened. If so he would definitely need to retain the best lawyer in the city. He reached in the console and instructed his phone to dial Shaleea. After multiple rings she didn't answer. He tried again, same thing. He dialed another number. Nikka picked up on the second ring.

"Hey Noah, wassup?" she asked in a groggy tone like she had been sleep.

"Nikka! Listen some shit popped off. I need to stay at ya crib tonight!"

"Okay but are you okay? Everything alright?"

"Yeah I'm good…Listen I can't say anything over the phone but I'm on my way there now…Have you talked to Shaleea?" he asked as he continued down the cracked city streets.

"No why?" she asked concerned, and now fully awake.

"She not picking up." Noah didn't want to go into details about him and Shaleea with Nikka. He just needed a safe place to stay until he figured out what his next move would be.

Over a week had passed and Noah hadn't heard anything from Shaleea. He didn't know what was going on and he was worried sick. After staying at Nikka's house for several days, Noah decided he was good to return home. Although people had heard the shots ring out, no one had come forward with information or told the police they saw anything. At least that was what he heard through his bartender acquaintance. He still wasn't sure how Nootie had found out he had put money on him and his siblings head. That was the only reason he could fathom Nootie gunning for him. Noah didn't deal with dudes who talked, so how they found out was still a mystery to him.

Noah didn't bother to call Shaleea again since her number had been recently changed. It just didn't make sense to him since everything in the house was still intact. She hadn't taken anything. He looked around and saw the still unpacked boxes strewn around the house. Once again his life was a mess and this time he wasn't even sure why. Several times he had called Gina as well as Shaleea's sisters, who told him not to worry since she was safe, but they too didn't know where she was. That didn't make any fucking sense to him. How could he not worry when she was five months pregnant with his child and seemed to have just disappeared?

Noah continued to look on at essentially nothing. He wanted to drink and smoke to take away the pressure on his mind but he couldn't. Being as though he just killed Nootie a little over a week ago he knew it was only a matter of time before his brother Teddy came looking for action.

He had to be on point and ready. He touched his waistline to make sure he was strapped. He was prepared either way. Just because he had a little money didn't mean he forgot what the streets was about. Yeah, he was ready.

ELEVEN

Shaleea

Shaleea paced her speed at sixty-five down the turnpike. Heaven was with her dad at his house in Jersey, and she was headed back to Philly for dinner at Naomi's house. Naomi had practically begged her to come by and fill her in on what was going on with her and why she was staying way out near the shore in Jersey.

Although her mom knew where she was as well as why, she made her promise not to tell the rest of her family. She would tell her sisters when she felt it was the right time. She didn't feel like hearing all the questions and *"I told you so's."* She also knew Shyanne looked at Noah like a big brother and would spill the beans if he pressed her.

Shaleea was focused on keeping her blood pressure and stress level down by relaxing and doing virtually nothing. Susan was handling the laundromats for her while she oversaw the paperwork remotely. Susan would scan and fax anything Shaleea requested. For the most part she had been in Jersey shopping, eating, and hearing old stories from her dad.

Shaleea took exit 6a for Philadelphia off the New Jersey Turnpike and after another thirty minutes of driving, she was at Naomi's Northeast Philadelphia home. Shaleea exited her car and approached the building. Naomi swung open the door before she could knock.

"Hey boo! I fucking missed you," she said, before giving Shaleea a big bear hug. Shaleea giggled. Naomi was always so hype.

"I missed you too," she replied. "It smells good. What we eating?" she asked greedily. Shaleea was famished after the nearly two hour ride.

"Girl I made some Chicken Fettuccini Alfredo with broccoli. Extra cheese and sauce, just how you like it." Shaleea smiled. She knew her well.

The two ladies sat down to eat and Naomi begged her to tell her what had been going on. Shaleea didn't really want to tell her the whole situation especially everything that led up to the move, but decided she would be completely honest with her close friend to free her burdened conscience.

Naomi hadn't brought up Mann since the day they ate lunch with Shameka. She had been seeing a new guy and often gushed about him so she figured Naomi was completely over thoughts of Mann. However, she thought wrong. After confessing to her that she and Mann had an encounter, as well as Noah finding out, Naomi stopped her right in mid-sentence.

"You fucked Mann?" she asked speechless. Her tone was laced with hate.

"Naomi we were drunk as fuck. He was so aggressive and shit just happened," she admitted, a little ashamed. She was hoping her friend wouldn't judge her entirely based off that one mistake.

"You knew I liked him though," she stated like a teenager, instead of the thirty year old woman she was. For some reason Shaleea expected her to be understanding, however Naomi wasn't trying to hear it from her friend, not even in her emotional pregnant state.

"That's trifling as fuck Leea. I was talking to the nigga and he was one of Noah's closest friends," she added.

"Look Naomi, at the end of the day what I did was wrong. I figured I would come to you and tell you like a woman instead of letting you find out any kind of way. You said yall were talking, but a couple phone calls and a double date doesn't exactly classify you two as an item. I don't have to sit here and lie about the nigga staring at me around my house, flirting with me, and he basically pushing himself on me when he felt he had the opportunity." Shaleea deliberately left out the part about her flirting hard too.

"He even came to the laundromat multiple times. He clearly was checking for me long before. I can't help that. What I did was wrong, yes. But do I think that stopped yall? No. If he was interested, he would've made something happen. You sure as hell was more than willing," Shaleea added, unintentionally making Naomi seem like a thirsty broad.

Naomi peered at Shaleea for a moment. Her long eyelashes seemed to flutter while she searched for a response.

"On some real shit, like I said before, you trifling. It's not enough for you to have a big ass house with a paid ass nigga. You want to fuck his friend too. Chicks like you kill me," she replied jealously.

"Why you sounding like a hater Naomi?" Shaleea asked puzzled, while calmly taking a sip of the iced tea Naomi had given her with dinner.

"I ain't no hater, I just can't stand chicks who got it all and it's never enough. Bitches like me who want a good dude, can't get one--"

Shaleea cut her off while she spoke. "What makes you think Noah's a good dude? Because he take care of me? Because he has money? Do you know what I go through? Dealing with the bitches he's fuckin or has fucked in the past," Shaleea asked, with her voice cracking. "A week ago I just had a bitch tell me she was six months pregnant by this nigga. That's why I left. That's why I went to my dad's in Jersey. My blood pressure soared through the roof and my pregnancy is in jeopardy.

So fuck all that good nigga shit," she said bluntly with tears lining the brim of her eyes.

"You just don't get it do you?" Naomi asked shaking her head, disregarding Shaleea's sob story. She would take Noah any day.

"I guess I don't. You know…maybe if you stop being so aggressive and coming across as desperate you would be able to get a good dude. Appearing thirsty is gonna have a nigga looking at you and ready to run. Maybe that's what happened with Mann…"

"No you fucked Mann that's what happened!" Naomi said, losing her patience. She had enough of her seemingly self-absorbed friend who was mentally attacking her and calling her thirsty in her own home.

"My fault? Girl bye. You was the same one letting the nigga watch you overeat at the crab truck and then throw the fuck up after piling liquor on top of it. You have some issues within yaself Naomi. That's why you can't get a man. Instead of trashing me and blaming me for allegedly stepping on ya toes, you need to address the real issues."

"Issues like what… my weight?" She was

asking Shaleea to confirm what she knew she was trying to say.

"Naomi you know what you're problems are. You don't need clarification from me. And frankly you make shit problems when they don't have to be. You're a beautiful girl despite your weight."

Naomi had far more than weight issues she was dealing with. She was also insecure because of her weight, which in turn was affecting her self-esteem. Although she knew she was attractive she also knew that she tried extra hard to get a man and it definitely came across as desperate. She was extremely envious of her friend. She had the babies, the man, and the house. Then she turns around and fucks someone who basically rejected her. To be rejected was enough, but to be rejected in lieu of her friend was even harder. To top it off Mann was smitten with Shaleea, damn near obsessing over the bitch like she was a treasure. It was a cold case of jealousy and it made Naomi angry and full of spite.

"Well Shaleea right now my problem is you and I think you should leave," she suggested.

"You putting me out ya house?" Shaleea asked Naomi in disbelief. When Naomi didn't respond, Shaleea grabbed her keys and began to leave. She looked back at Naomi but she had walked off to her bedroom. Shaleea knew what she did was wrong but Naomi had come from a completely different angle. She always thought her friend was happy for her, not jealous. The more time passed, the more she was learning people were never who they portrayed themselves to be; herself included.

Noah

Noah pushed the sheet off his brown, chiseled body and got out of the bed. After throwing on a t-shirt and basketball shorts he went downstairs to deactivate the alarm. Although it wasn't that late he was in bed trying to rest his tired, sleep deprived body. He had just received a call from Naomi stating that she had some information about Shaleea. One of the handful of people he reached out to initially when looking for her, he felt a sense of relief when she called him.

Noah still didn't know what was going on with Shaleea but he was hoping Naomi could tell him that tonight. He watched as the headlights of Naomi's Toyota Camry lit up the front of the house, announcing her arrival.

After opening the door and allowing her in, he headed to the kitchen so he could pour a light drink and find out what she knew.

"Thanks for calling me....So wassup?" he asked, while taking a small sip of rum and coke he had poured.

"Well Shaleea called me and she's okay. She's in Jersey at her dad's house."

"Why the fuck would she be all the way up there?" he asked with raised brows.

"Eve called her...She supposed to be like six months pregnant or something?" she asked Noah.

Noah shook his head from side to side and immediately grew angry. He should've known Eve was behind Shaleea leaving.

"The bitch is lying," he stated calmly, sitting his glass down on the granite countertop in the kitchen. "What doesn't make sense to me is why Shaleea would just pick up and leave. She usually would've came to me and talked to me."

"When Eve called her she was at the doctor's office. Her blood pressure was high and thee baby was at risk...Noah honey, I don't think she's coming back," she added for finality. Naomi didn't know for sure if Shaleea was coming back but was hoping Noah would respond the way she wanted him to.

Noah took a deep breath and let everything she said sink in. He couldn't believe the bullshit he just heard. "Thanks Naomi. At least I know she's ok." He tried to give her quick hug to express his gratitude and assumed she would leave afterward. However, when he hugged her she didn't let go. Instead he felt her lips pressed against his neck and her tongue slither across it causing a jolt to his dick. Naomi pressed her big, soft body against his.

"Yo, what are you doing?" he asked, pushing her away. He looked at her and lust filled her eyes. He couldn't help but also notice sadness and desperation.

"Noah baby, Shaleea's not coming back. I can take her place. Nobody has to know," she said, approaching him and rubbing his chest, her left hand sliding down to the bulge in his pants.

"Yo are you fucking crazy. What the fuck is wrong with you bitches?! Get out!" he stated, surprising her. He had enough shit to deal with and her fat ass wanted to make it worse. Shaleea was gonna bring her ass home and fucking Naomi behind her back was sure to eliminate that if she found out. He was tired of the games. It wasn't worth it. No bitch was. Noah wasn't sure what caused Naomi to come with the treachery but he wasn't taking the bait.

Naomi just stared at Noah and felt like less of a woman even more. Not only was she rejected by Mann for Shaleea, she was also rejected by Noah. She practically threw herself on him and he still didn't want to touch her. It was too much for Naomi. The jealousy she possessed for her friend had surfaced full force and she knew their friendship was essentially over. She quickly spun around and fled the house embarrassed. Noah huffed in aggravation before pouring himself another drink and throwing on his black Jordan Retros. He was about to go out and take care of some shit he should have been handled.

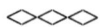

Noah parked his Range Rover around the corner

from the shabby chain hotel and took the back steps to the room he visited Eve in on multiple occasions. The past year she had mostly stayed in the same room at the same hotel, so she wasn't hard to locate. Although it was May it was still a cool night so Noah felt confident about wearing his hoodie without looking suspicious. He knocked on the door and waited for Eve to answer.

"Who is it?" she called. Noah didn't respond. "Who is it?" she asked again. Still no response. "Aight well you gon stay the fuck out there," she informed the unidentified visitor.

Noah calmly waited at the door. He wasn't going to knock again. He didn't want people looking out their doors being nosey. He knew Eve was going to open the door eventually. She was just as nosey as anyone else and would eventually want to see who was at the door.

Just as he suspected, the bolts started to unlock on the door as Eve's curiosity won against her common sense and safety instincts. As soon as she opened the door Noah forced himself inside with an aggressive push. The force caused Eve to stumble back and fall on the floor.

"Bitch what the fuck I tell you," he snarled, approaching her in his dark hoodie like the grim reaper. Eve was too frightened to speak so she remained quiet.

"Oh you don't have shit to say now right...But ya lil stinkin ass had a whole lot to say when you fucking called my girl!" he said cocking back his foot and kicking her in the legs. Pain shot through her body causing her to scream out.

"Shut the fuck up," he said, grabbing a handful of her weave and standing her up against him. Her head was tilted back at an odd angle since he was holding her hair and tears were forming in her eyes. She didn't recognize this man.

"Noah please let me go. I'm pregnant, please."

"Bitch, I don't give a fuck! Fuck you and that fucking baby," he spat without compassion.

He violently pushed her onto the dusty mattress. Seizing the opportunity to defend herself, she grabbed the lamp that was nearby on the nightstand and hurled it at him. Noah ducked and it crashed into the wall. Rage overcame him and he rushed over to the bed and grabbed her by her throat. He was sick of her and wished he had never met her. She had caused so much trouble when he had done nothing more than be honest from the rip. He just wanted to do the right thing now but everyone was out for themselves. Everyone was willing to use him as a pawn to achieve satisfaction for themselves. He was going to put an end to this shit tonight with everyone. He didn't give a fuck about the consequences when they surfaced. He had plenty of money to clean up even the biggest mess.

He used both hands to apply immense pressure to Eve's throat. She kicked and squirmed on the bed but he was too strong. While they struggled, melancholy overcame him and he zoned out. Noah saw his former life flash before his eyes as he stood over Eve with his hands wrapped around her throat. He thought of all that he had, and all that his life was, before her scheming ass had come into the picture. He cursed the day he had met her. Instead of his surroundings, he saw nothing but red through his pupils. The sounds she made became muffled and distant. Noah's heart beat rapidly and before he realized it, he had completely blacked out. It was too late.

Noah let go and Eve was no longer moving.

He stared at her for a moment and his hate tempted him to spit on her. However, he wasn't about to leave fresh DNA for the cops. He had money to clean up a mess, but he wasn't stupid either. Reality quickly set in for Noah and he realized he had to get the fuck out of there. Eve was dead and he was about to go the fuck to prison if he didn't jet.

Noah backed away and slowly opened the door. He turned the knob and quietly peeped out the door. The coast was clear so he made a brisk exit into the hallway and headed for the stairs. He didn't care about fingerprints since his would be one of many in the highly traveled room. As Noah fled the scene and headed back to his truck around the corner, Bianca who was down the hall, emerged from her own room and went to go check on her friend.

Bianca had heard the sounds and figured Eve may had fell. She had no idea Eve wasn't alone. Bianca knocked on the door and called out, "Eve open the door bitch, it's Bianca." When there was no response she grew worried.

Turning the knob, she realized the door wasn't locked. She entered the room and the scene in front of her caused her to spring into action.

"Eve!" she called, running over to her friend who was laying limp on the bed appearing lifeless. She didn't know how to check a pulse so she felt her chest to see if her heart was beating and then stuck her hand under Eve's nose to see if she was breathing. Bianca immediately began screaming for help.

"Help me!!" she yelled, before grabbing the motel phone and calling 911.

"911 what's your emergency?" they asked.

"My friend isn't breathing and I can't feel her heart beat! I found her like this! Please help me and hurry! She's pregnant!"

"Try to calm down ma'am. Can you tell me where you are?"

"At the Sleep Inn on Roosevelt Boulevard in Philadelphia! Please hurry!" she frantically demanded while checking Eve's chest again.

"Try to stay calm ma'am. Help is on the way."

TWELVE

Mann

Mann was pissed when he found out Nootie was the person they found outside of the Clock Bar. He didn't give a fuck about him being dead, what bothered him is that Noah wasn't and he had paid Nootie's simple, unreliable ass $5,000. He wasn't gon sweat it though. He was just gonna throw some more money on his head.

Mann continued to cruise down Old York Road in his new BMW and stared at all the prostitutes who lined up the streets. His mom used to work the same strip. He watched them try to wave down car after car, with one finally stopping an elderly suitor looking for a quick sexual fix.

He shook his head and silently wished he could open fire on the whole block without going to jail. He hated prostitutes, especially strung out ones who chose to neglect their children for a temporary feeling of nostalgia.

Mann turned into Hunting Park and made his way to the parking area for a game of hoops. A couple nigga's from his team were meeting down there to shoot the shit and smoke weed. Everybody hung out at the park when there wasn't shit to do, and paid niggas like himself were like God's when they pulled up.

As Mann pulled into the park he just so happened to glance over to Cayuga Street that was parallel to the park. He spotted his young nigga Slay who slung weed for him, posted up at the window of an SUV. When Mann looked closely he realized it was Noah in his Range Rover.

Mann immediately grabbed his gun. He figured he wouldn't get a second chance. Mann continued up and headed out the park. He figured he would bend the block and come from behind since Noah was facing the opposite way. After stopping to a light Mann turned onto 10th street and u-turned onto Cayuga Street. He slowly crept down the block where Noah's truck was parked.

Mann slowed his speed and retrieved his gun off the seat when he got close to Noah's truck. He rolled down the window and his young nigga pointed to him and mouthed some words. Mann immediately opened fire.

Pop! Pop! Pop!

Noah

Noah was sitting in his running truck talking to a young nigga he had met through Mann name Slay. He had seen the youngin and inquired about Mann's whereabouts. Slay hadn't seen him in a few days but surprisingly while they talked he pointed to the street and said, "There he go right there."

As Noah turned to face the street he spotted Mann with his gun extended out the window. Everything happened quickly after that.

Pop! Pop! Pop! Mann fired repeatedly into Noah's truck, instantly killing Slay with a random bullet to the eye. Noah tried to duck but the bullets tore through the interior of his Range Rover. He frantically grabbed the handle as the bullets continued to rain down into and on the truck. He felt a bullet rip through his stomach during his struggle to escape. The pain was enough to bring him to his knees.

Noah managed to get the door open and as he slid out of the car he felt another bullet tear into his back. His entire lower body instantly went numb as he tumbled to the hard pavement. The shots eventually stopped and Noah heard Mann peel down the block, leaving nothing more than the smell of burnt rubber behind, along with two fallen bodies.

Noah could no longer feel the pain as he slipped out of consciousness. He watched his blood coat the ground and he eventually faded out, gun still attached to his hip.

THIRTEEN

Shaleea

Shaleea got the call from her mom nearly one in the morning that Noah had been shot. Luckily she wasn't far. After Naomi put her out, she didn't feel like driving back to New Jersey so she was close by at a room in downtown Philadelphia.

Noah had been transported by paramedics to Temple Hospital and that was pretty much all her mom had told her. Since Noah didn't have her new number, the police contacted his next of kin. Gina's name was listed under Mom in Noah's phone so they contacted her first. Shaleea's sisters, Gina, Chris, and Tate were all headed to the hospital. Gina had called everyone. It didn't look good.

Shaleea pulled up to the hospital and illegally parked in front of the Emergency Room. They could tow the car for all she cared. Her concern was Noah. Running to the check in desk, she quickly began talking.

"I'm here for Noah Thomas. Is he okay? I'm Shaleea Smith, his fiancé," she stated out of breath. Her heart was racing a mile a minute and nausea enveloped her.

"Give me one minute ma'am. He just came in," the older black lady at the desk told her. She quickly looked through the computers before getting up and heading to the back. She only was gone a minute, but to Shaleea it felt like hours. She was beginning to get light headed. The suspense was killing her. She wanted to know what happened. She didn't know where he had been shot, if he was okay, who he was with, nothing.

The lady soon returned, but she was accompanied by an African American, silver haired distinguished looking doctor with blue scrubs.

"Miss Smith?" he asked.

"I'm Miss Smith, Noah's fiancée, is he okay?"

The doctor looked at her solemnly and carefully chose his words.

"Noah was shot multiple times, once in the stomach and once in his back. The bullet to his back damaged his spinal cord. The doctors are doing everything they can to save his life right now....But to be honest the chances of him surviving are slim....If he does survive he will most likely be paralyzed for the remainder of his life."

Shaleea put her hand to her chest and tried to digest what the doctor said. It was too much. The hospital was too bright; the lights in the ceiling too hot. She felt faint and fell to the floor. She thought she would pass out but she didn't.

"Are you okay?" the doctor asked her, crouching down to take a look at her. "Get a wheelchair," he yelled, after getting a glimpse of her blood soaked leg.

"Ma'am, how many months are you?" he asked in a serious, authoritative tone.

"I'm five, ughhhh!" she yelled. Pain unexpectedly shot through her abdomen.

"Get her to the back! Hurry up!" he yelled.

"Ughhhh!" she screamed again when she felt

pain rip through her body. This time she felt it in her back. Shaleea felt warm water running down her leg and knew she was going in labor.

"Oh my god, oh my god!" she screamed. "My baby's coming! It's too soon, please make him stop!" she yelled.

Several nurses rushed out to assist and tried to calm Shaleea down. She felt faint again. Bright lights flashed in front of her face, her chest felt heavy and next thing you know she lost consciousness.

Shaleea was heavily sedated to manage her pain but she was able to recognize the doctor when he walked into the room. Gina, Chris, and Tate surrounded her bedside as she blinked her heavy eyes and tried to make out what the doctor was saying. She couldn't determine whether they were talking about Noah or her baby. Finally gathering up enough energy to speak, she whispered out in a faint voice, "Where's my baby." She didn't remember much but she did know that she was forced to deliver her baby early.

With tears flooding her eyes, Gina shook her

head from left to right and responded with her voice trembling, "Shaleea baby...I'm sorry honey, he didn't make it."

Shaleea closed her eyes and the pain she felt took her breath away. It was like a mack truck had hit her in her chest. The pain was truly indescribable. Her baby boy was dead. She hadn't even had the honor of meeting him yet. With tears streaming from her face, she asked, "Is Noah okay?" Her heart ached in her heaving chest.

Gina looked at Chris, and Chris glanced at Tate. Tate nodded his head for her to go ahead and tell Shaleea.

"I'm sorry baby but...," she cried out. She threw her head into her palms and sobbed. It was all too much for Gina and she had no idea how Shaleea was going to cope. Her family would see her through...

Deceit, Lies, & Alibi's III: The Finale
COMING: AUGUST 2015

Shaleea's strength is put to the ultimate test in this final installment of **Deceit, Lies, & Alibi's.** Everyone has a breaking point and she finally reaches hers when a legal situation emerges and a new person comes into the picture. Will Shaleea be able to handle a humbling disability, legal issues, and a new person that will change her life forever? Find out, in Deceit, Lies, & Alibi's 3.

Please leave a rating or review.

Look out for Deceit, Lies, & Alibi's 3. The FINAL book of the series.

Email me for the release date along with questions or comments at uptownshontaiye@yahoo.com.

Email "GIVEAWAYS" to uptownbookspublication@yahoo.com. We have giveaways monthly. (Free books, and prizes for readers on our mailing list.)

Made in the USA
Middletown, DE
29 February 2016